AFTER FRANK
A FAIRY TALE

AFTER FRANK
A FAIRY TALE

VIVIENNE WOOLF

GAINSBOROUGH HOUSE PRESS
LONDON • CHICAGO, IL

First published in 2019 by Gainsborough House Press

Copyright © 2019 Vivienne Woolf

British Library Cataloguing in Publication Data

ISBN 978 1 909719 17 0 (Cloth)
ISBN 978 1 909719 16 3 (Paper)
ISBN 978 1 909719 18 7 (Kindle)
ISBN 978 1 909719 15 6 (Ebook)

Library of Congress Cataloging in Publication Data

Printed by Independent Publishers Group, Chicago, IL, USA

CONTENTS

ACKNOWLEDGEMENTS

Thank you to Shelley Weiner, Harriet Horne, Carolyn Nicholson and Tracey Waples. Thank you to Sally Hyman for the beautiful cover illustration. Most of all, thank you to my husband, David for his unstinting encouragement and love.

AFTER FRANK

'In the disquiet of these days I carry you with me deep within
my pocket, at the bottom of my footfall, in every cloud
that brushes by.'

Kylie Johnson

PREFACE: 2000

Rose and Frank Rosin spend their forty-seventh wedding anniversary eating marrow cake on a beach while the sun sets over the English Channel. The year is 2000 and the world has entered a new phase.

In all the time they've known each other, Frank has not been away from Rose for a single night and this thought passes from her to him as the moon rises in the sky.

'You're more angel than man to me now,' she says, 'what's in this world for us beside each other?'

'Olive,' he replies.

Rose is a petite, nervous woman with curly hair which she dyes the blonde of her childhood and which grows like a wave on top of her head. She's inherited her mother Edith's long fingers and wears the wedding ring which belonged to her, but has green eyes to her mother's brown, is agitated where her mother is self-contained, talkative where Edith is silent and smiles only when Rose enters a room.

Rose has only one photograph of her father and it's of him standing behind his seated wife with a hand on her shoulder. One morning, he ate his breakfast and went out waving and never came back nor told his wife and daughter where he was going or why. All Rose has to remember him by – apart from the photograph -are two watercolours he painted; one of a sunset and one of a tree and she never stops yearning for him.

Rose can't get on with mascara but never leaves home without dabbing on Dusky Rose lipstick and blusher to match and re-applies both as often as needed to rescue the remnants of a once beautiful face.

She loves sunshine and always lifts her face in the direction of the sun.

'I love days when I can smell the sunshine on my roses,' she tells anyone who cares to listen, 'but I don't fare so well on wintry days when darkness settles in before you know it, locks me indoors and wipes away the sun.'

Because the sky's colour affects her moods, she dresses like the weather. When it rains, she wears black or grey and when the sun shines brightly and makes her want to cartwheel around her flower beds, she wears a yellow coat or orange skirt. Whatever the weather, she wears wellington boots over her shoes 'to save them'.

I become a different, more confident person in my boots, she thinks, and she often imagines herself in her boots with secateurs in hand and covered only in sunlight. She pushes this image to the back of her mind and never shares it with Frank.

My thoughts have a mind of their own, she thinks, I must be careful.

Frank is a carpenter, built as solid as Rose is light and is as stubborn as the wood he carves. He comes from the north where winters are harsh, seas rough and summers short and he travelled down south to seek work. His father and grandfather, who were carpenters before him, bequeathed him their lathes, their aprons, their poverty and their love of the sea.

His hair is the colour of sand, he has one blue-green eye like spring and one brown one like winter but it's his hands with their prominent veins which first attracted Rose.

'There's an understanding between your hands and the wood you work with. They just get on with it,' she tells him and her eyes seldom leave his hands. 'Your hands always smell of sawdust and I've come to know them as my own. From the moment I saw them, a part of me left to settle in you and will stay there for the rest of time. You've the handsomest hands in the world.'

PROLOGUE: THE PAST

Rose and Frank met at school and immediately fell in love. When they were twenty-three, Frank proposed to Rose in his Morris Minor where they sat eating Neapolitan ice creams on a rainy afternoon.

Frank said, 'Rose, you're the smell of a rainbow, the breeze through trees and the promise of sunshine. Without you, I'd be as lonely as a lighthouse and I'll love you till the sea loses its waves.'

Rose said, 'I don't know how you speak as you do or know what you know, but when pieces of me are scattered, you put them together again.'

Because the engine was running so the wipers could do their work, Frank proposed twice. 'Shall we join together Rose?' he shouted, 'shall we join together?'

Rose rubbed a blob of ice cream off the corner of her mouth and agreed to be his wife and they sat there holding hands till the sun dropped into the sea.

He produced from a pouch the ring Edith had given him when he'd asked her prior permission.

'I'm happy as lapping water at low tide,' he said as he slipped it onto one of Rose's long fingers.

'Me too,' she replied as the lace of her sleeve brushed the hair on his arm. 'I trust you – and that's something.'

Because she believed in angels, she added, 'If you look at the sky and don't make a sound, you'll see angels all around us like clouds.'

Frank asked her to describe an angel for he may well have seen one and mistaken it for a cloud.

'I think I see one,' he said when she didn't reply.

He never stopped believing that clouds were clouds even if he wanted this not to be the case but his first gift to her was a wooden angel he had carved with wings outspread and hands held together in prayer and he left it on her pillow. He drew a sailing boat on the note attached and wrote her name on the sail.

They married in a registry office in the spring of the following year. It was a simple affair. The sun shone out of a profound blue sky and she wore a pink lace dress with a sprig of cherry blossom in her hair. He was embarrassed to find a spring of the same in his button hole while her only regret was that she couldn't find him a pink rose. They ate chicken, beans and potatoes from the garden, the wedding cake was made from marrows and shaped like an angel and they danced under the stars.

They moved into the house in the centre of the town in which Rose was born. Her father had built it and, to begin with, they shared it with Edith, together with her ornaments and furniture which included a vase of porcelain roses and a rocking chair.

'Home, for me, is anywhere I feel your arm around my waist,' Frank told Rose.

'I can't imagine a life without you,' she replied and felt as calm and content as roses in sunshine.

On days off, Frank drove to the sea and walked up and down the shore – whatever the weather, counting his steps and lost in a dream world of water and sand. He seldom spoke about his work but when he did, he said, 'When my wood comes to life, I feel the roll of the earth right here in its grain. We have no more right to the earth than anyone else, but my wood shows me its power.'

'Cheers to the earth, cheers to wood, Frank, and cheers to life,' replied Rose, who felt his words to be like sunshine.

Their shared house preoccupied them. It stood in a narrow terrace of differently coloured houses which looked look like a rainbow come to life in bricks and mortar and they painted it the blue-green of one of Frank's eyes.

Edith filled the garden with potatoes, beans and marrows which she placed in long straight rows. Frank's contribution was an olive tree which he chose because its wood is strong and durable and good for carving. Rose planted roses wherever there were gaps. When Frank returned from work, smelling of sawdust, he touched his tree and took in the roses' perfume and all was right with the world.

While Frank was in his workshop, Rose gardened, baked or read love stories with serious concentration. Edith worked in the local library and Rose took the bus there every Wednesday, returning with a load of books in her bag.

For the first sixteen years of their marriage, it was as if nothing stood in their way – either that or they didn't ask for much. They lived a happy enough life even if she sometimes wondered why he was so taciturn and they never spoke about having children.

Then, in their fortieth year on earth, a baby girl slid feet first down Rose's birth canal on an autumn morning after a night when an electric storm blew all the petals off Rose's roses and the leaves of the olive tree on to the windows of their house.

'I have given birth to an angel,' said Rose, who felt she'd somehow known her baby from another time.

'What are we going to call her?' asked Frank who remained unsure about angels.

'Olive,' she replied, looking at the tree.

He smiled.

He lifted his baby into the air, 'one, two, three, little Olive, here we go,' he said and found what he'd been waiting for all this time. He was an only child, Rose was an only child and here was their only child but when the midwife put her hands together and thanked God for bringing this child to them, her tone was so firmly reassuring, no-one was reassured.

If Frank and Rose said goodbye to their former life, they felt love for their daughter she needed to do nothing to deserve; everything revolved around the baby whose favourite thing was being near the sea.

At the end of each day, Rose drove Olive to the sea, tucked blankets around her and pushed her along the promenade to watch the sun colour the water pink and see seabirds dive across the waves.

Rose tilted her face so she could feel the sun's last warmth and she swung her baby up to the fading light and sang the Nina Simone songs Edith had sung in the same place and in the same melancholy voice which had taken people by surprise but which had felt to Rose like waves melting into sand.

'Summertime, and the livin' is easy. Fish are jumpin' and the cotton is high. Oh, your daddy's rich and your ma is good-lookin'. So hush, little baby, don't you cry,' Rose sang.

When the sky turned black, she drove back to the blue-green house where salt seeped into furniture, curtains were tossed about like sails and Frank sat waiting with his soft eyes on the door because all it took for his eyes to light up was for Rose and Olive to return.

When her parents discovered that Olive walked in a strange way, stepping forward on to her right foot and dragging her left foot behind her, they were on the beach. The sun was shining and Olive was taking her time because she loved her life.

Rose had been studying Olive's walk as if watching a film in slow motion.

'Do you see Frank? Watch Olive walk. It's terrible to watch things fall apart. Do you see?' she said, struggling to find words which expressed her thoughts which were busy jumping about like the rolling sea.

'Yes, I see,' said Frank who didn't see anything fall apart or find cause for concern. 'Things change like the tides and there is nothing you can do to stop this. Olive came feet first into the world so she could stand strong like any other. There will always be those who won't see past her feet and will think of her as no more than the sum of what can be said about her, but Olive is fine – however she walks. She'll grow up like the rest of us. She will have no choice.'

'I wonder,' mused Rose.

'You wonder what?' asked Frank who still saw her as his high school sweetheart whom he found charming, but innocent.

Time passed and Olive grew – watched closely by her parents. Most afternoons she sat on the floor of Frank's workshop, insulated from other people with her feet in socks for, whatever the weather, she wasn't allowed to go barefoot in the workshop. Frank didn't speak to her but kept his gaze on her face while she stacked wood shavings into orderly piles and laughed at him because he wore an apron over his trousers and coaxed wood into strange shapes. Nothing could go wrong for her when Frank was around.

It wasn't until Olive attended school that she was forced to confront the different ways her disability was experienced by others. She felt lonely and misunderstood and her classmates were wary of her. It was clear from the start that she wasn't stupid, but schooling failed to interest her. She had little aptitude for learning and felt there was no point to most of the things they made her do. Beyond being careful around her – for they never understood her reasons for doing things, her teachers left her untroubled. Her classmates were wary of her, too. Olive was the girl others mocked, hiding their smiles behind their hands, making her feel different and inadequate or calling her Olive Raisin. When her back was turned, some even imitated her walk.

Frank, who hadn't stayed long in school would ask, 'what went on in school, Olive?' as if his asking would bring him the learning he lacked.

'I don't know why everything is different for me than for others,' she replied.

'Be glad you are just like yourself,' answered Rose, who struggled with the fact that she, herself, couldn't compete with younger, livelier mothers.

Where Olive did excel was in all things relating to numbers. It was as if God was trying to make it up to her for her foot. Olive found comfort in numbers. She loved numbers so much that complex patterns of numbers often covered the landscapes of her dreams. She measured things and measured them down to the last fraction of a centimetre. Fours, fives, sevens, tens, fifty-eights, eighty-threes – all assumed lives of their own and no time passed as happily for her as the time she spent stacking, jumbling and re-assembling numbers.

'My strange walk doesn't show when I'm adding and subtracting,' Olive told her parents.

Rose continued to worry about what people were saying. Most days, she busied herself with books or cakes or roses and acted as if nothing were wrong and she loved her child for carrying on when she thought others might have given up. But there were days when Rose felt conscious of her limitations. She stayed in her bed, staring into space or watching smoke rise from her cigarettes, oppressed by a sense of needing to do something without knowing what this something should be. Sometimes she looked out of her window in the hope that the clouds might bring her clarity but when none came, she pored over horoscopes in order to try to unearth the world inside her child.

When she turned sixteen, Olive refused to return to school. She surprised herself by announcing this to her parents as she hadn't planned to do so. She took to walking instead. As a child, she had often dreamed of being an adult, and although her dreams were vague, in them she was usually walking.

Now, because of her limp, she walked in a deceptively bouncy way but there was no bounce in her plan. She had no plan. She pulled on a coat, put wellington boots over her shoes 'to save them' and dragged her left foot behind her as she went. She walked when the air was full of salt, she walked out under rainbows, she walked out to marvel at the changing seasons, she walked out at the pause between day and night, and she walked when the skies were so dark all she could see were stray cats' eyes and television sets flickering behind net curtains. Everything was beautiful to her when she walked.

She didn't try to find new places, but tried, instead, to find people, a person - herself, perhaps, or to come upon her father who had given her his assurance that there was education to be found from people other than teachers.

Very often she would start walking and find herself miles away from home – past the brightly coloured houses around the quay, past hollyhocks, rhododendrons and hydrangeas, past the library, bed and breakfast houses, antique shops, pound stores, cafes, wine bars, a church and charity outlets until she reached a little wooden house Frank had built near rocks above the ocean where the air was thick and damp. She took off her boots and shoes and clambered down the rocks into the water so she could watch the waves and feel gravel and shells tickle her toes.

I am not like others, she thought.

When she began to tower above her parents, their house and garden with its rosebushes and olive tree changed for her for ever. On one of her walks it came to her that she wasn't going to live with them all her life, but hat she was going to live in the wooden house Frankhad built and that she would never return home.

She made her second big announcement, 'I am leaving home.'

Again, she probably didn't intend this. She probably didn't mean this. But, having made the declaration, her words took strength and coiled themselves around her like a rope which tied her to their meaning.

'The wooden house is there, anyway, Olive was beside me when I built it and I've prepared her by walking the journey between the houses with her many times. I've also told her stories of people who have left home and survived,' Frank explained to Rose.

On an ordinary day in June when the sun shone in the watery way it can in the northern hemisphere, Olive draped her shawl around her shoulders and walked away from the house of her birth to begin living her life in the wooden house overlooking the gentle, sandy beach – rare for these parts – which separated her from her parents.

Because Olive had left home many times before that to spend nights on the rocks or the beach and because she moved in and out so frequently, Rose and Frank were sure she would be back. But on this day, Olive felt able to kiss Rose on the cheek, pack her bags and walk away from her room with its wire hangers, sea green curtains and views of rose beds and an olive tree.

'Where now – and why?' asked Rose, who knew, of course, about the house near the rocks.

'I want to,' replied Olive, stubborn as her father.

At the start, it wasn't clear even to Olive that she had moved out. She couldn't say she was preparing for her future – or, at least, for her next step because it was difficult for her to come to terms with the intrusion this thought represented. She couldn't explain that everything at home remained precious to her. She couldn't explain that she didn't leave until she had said goodbye to every space in the house and she couldn't explain that the courage it took to leave her parents had cost her.

All she could explain was that a wave of something had passed over her and was driving her on so she took along her cat and as many of her possessions as she could, including a wooden angel Frank had carved, some clothes, a few pieces of furniture, a recent photograph of her standing between her parents and a cloth Edith had embroidered with the words 'if the sky had no tears, the world would have no rainbows.'

'I collect rainbows in my head,' she told her parents because she remembered when and where she had seen most of them, 'even if they're there and then gone – like life.'

'I think it's terrific that you're making your way on your own,' said Frank, fearing that the alternative to her leaving might be unhappiness and surprising Rose with this statement because she imagined both he and Olive hated change.

'I understand why you need to leave but leave quickly – that would be best – and don't turn back or think that what's left behind is better than what's in front because it is not,' he stated.

He lied to Rose, 'she doesn't need us anymore. She's moving only two miles away, anyway,' and this brought all conversation about the move to an end.

Rose waved cheerily to Olive's back and walked behind her at the start of her journey, following the marks her feet left on the sand.

'Watch out Olive,' she called, 'the tide covers the sand twice a day.' To her credit, she did not cry, 'Olive, come back.'

Then she returned to her home and her roses and lit a cigarette with as much abandon as she could.

'There goes my life walking across the beach,' she told Frank, 'I hope she doesn't lose her angel. You know I'm superstitious. Thank goodness she doesn't suffer from sea-sickness. She might come home when she has had enough.' Then she asked, 'what have we done?'

'Nothing,' he replied.

Rose kept every trace of her daughter which remained in the house-which was a pair of shoes and a school cardigan and for months after her departure, she resorted to speaking to the Olive who lived in her head. Her photograph album filled something of the space Olive had occupied for, in it, she found her child again, standing on a beach or with her hand on the back of a cat.

Their first night alone was the worst. When Rose shut her door on the dark, she could almost see the silence. She stared at the patch on the wall where Edith's embroidered cloth had hung and into the empty cupboard where coat hangers jangled and dust lined the floor. She walked around and around like someone who has just been told she should unlearn everything she has previously learned.

The image of Olive in her green shawl floated into her head and her tired mind pictured her daughter lying in darkness on the floor of her new home. She quickly pushed the image away and, instead, sent waves of longing lapping Olive's way.

What had Olive felt about the day's activities? she wondered as she went outside to water and weed, plant and prune and inspect her roses under the stars. What life is she planning?

At the other end of the bay – and only a beach away from her parents, Olive lay down on the floor of her new home with no plans except to share her life with her cat and live as if it were commonplace to be sleeping and eating in a house set upon rocks close to the sea. She was tired. She had spent a good part of the day walking up and down the beach and had used up every bit of her strength to come this far. She had folded four pairs of trousers, two blouses, a green cardigan, a beige dress with patterns of flamingos on it which made it look like a work of art and a few green shawls and put them in a corner. She had hung Edith's embroidered cloth above a chest piled full of Frank's carvings – including the angel and had placed the photograph of herself and her parents looking happy on top of it.

She surveyed her space until it grew dark, owls began hooting from faraway treetops and all she could see were the silver buckles on her sandals and – through her windows, the white tips of the waves.

She thought about the olive tree and about Rose's roses which smelled of sunshine and had leaves so green they were almost blue and she knew she had left them not to run away – because she would never run away – but to move towards something else and she set to waiting for that something else to take shape.

1

2001

On a sunny Wednesday at five past eleven in the morning when the sky is filled with white aeroplane trails, Frank dies of a heart attack while seated in his car. He understood people and situations Rose could not and found meaning in life where she could not, but he leaves her on the day they bury Edith.

Rose and Olive go into the house to make sandwiches after Edith's funeral and when they come out to find Frank, seagulls are screeching overhead, and he is dead. He is seventy-two, Rose is seventy-two and Olive is thirty-two.

'Frank has died without warning,' cries Rose whose mother died the week previously.

She finds the heap that is her husband slumped over the steering wheel with his cap on his head, his grey coat unbuttoned and his boots smelling of the sea.

'Frank is definitely dead,' she tells Olive who stands limply beside her. 'When I think back on things, he has been lean and alone and silent for a while now and all he has wanted to do is lie down and wait for the day to end. I shall never get the chance to say, "you can die now, Frank, I'll be fine" or "we've made it to fifty" or a simple "thank you Frank." I always thought I'd be the first to go with my fluttering heart and offbeat ways, but life has a funny way of ending before you have finished your business.'

She tries to remember what the three of them talked about on the way to Edith's funeral – something ordinary like the weather or lunch or weeds and her first concern is that Frank's boots are dirty.

'This is easier for me to think about than the fact that he is dead,' she explains.

When the full realisation does hit, the wish to run back to her mother's grave and have things turn out differently, breaks over her like a wave.

'What have we done?' asks Olive who has difficulty remembering, at first, that Frank loved her, that he taught her things she treasures knowing and that he never asked for anything she wasn't able to do or give.

'My life always pointed towards him like a boat sailing to harbour,' she continues. 'Now that he's gone, everything will change. I'll go on walking, I'll go on counting my steps, but no amount of walking or counting will bring him back. The only comforting thought is that the sea will be there whether he is alive or not.'

She reflects on the fact that she's younger than he was when she was born. Her thirty-two years have little in common with his; she hasn't married or had a child and has never left the town of her birth.

'When I think about it, my life seems to be only partly that of a grown woman,' she tells Rose.

As she predicts, everything does change.

Olive has the wooden house, so Frank bequeaths Rose his lathe, aprons and his workshop which she sells quite quickly. He doesn't leave much money and Rose can't be doing with his love the sea.

Still, I have my house, I live frugally and grow most of my own food. Olive will never go hungry while I live in the town, she thinks.

Although she never fully reveals the details of Frank's passing, she tells anyone who cares to listen, 'a week ago I was a very different woman.'

Frank's funeral is held on a rainy Friday. The things which mattered to him are locked inside him, but they bury him with his boots which still smell of wood and the sea. Because he had a comfortable acquaintance with almost everyone, most of the people in the town turn up although there are a lot Rose and Olive don't know.

At a time of death you need someone to tell you what to do, but no-one warned Olive about the sadness which comes over her when Frank's body enters the ground. She scans people's faces hoping to recognize someone she knows before shovelling the first clump of soil on to the grave.

Her heart contracts with every sob which comes from Rose's chest but when the minister speaks, his words crawl all over her like sea snakes and make her shiver.

'Frank was, in his way, an inspiration, a humble man, a man of the sea he loved so much...' the minister rambles on. His puzzled, melancholy expression, hands which flop all over the place and the fact that he's almost shamelessly examining Rose's dyed blonde hair make little impact on Olive.

Dragonflies start buzzing around the grave as Rose bows her head in prayer and patterns of numbers begin to bloom in Olive's head.

While it felt like Frank was around as long as the sea, his share of my life was small. Going forward, the sum of my years on earth will be missing the sum of my father's and this is difficult to bear, she thinks. Olive then rounds up all the mourners in her mind and arranges them according to age.

She continues to scan her life. 'My father lived little more than twice as long as I,' she says but no-one hears except Rose, perhaps, and the rain which washes Olive's words away, leaving her looking as if she's mouthing silently to herself.

There's no reason why I should say anything further, she thinks.

Rose makes out only the 'twice as long' and then nothing. She is prone to anxiety about Olive's physical and mental health and sometimes feels inexplicably guilty about her daughter's birth and the fact that she came out feet first. She tries to reply.

'It's hard for me to know what to say right now except that there must be a pattern to things even when they don't seem to make sense.'

She adjusts the shawl around Olive's shoulders because there is a wind blowing and it's full of salt. She moves closer to Olive so she can share her umbrella and she hopes her use of the word 'pattern' has helped.

The colour of this shawl does nothing for Olive's skin, she thinks.

Olive stares back at her like at someone whose name she has forgotten.

Rose holds her breath as Olive appears to be hovering on the brink of speech. 'Did you say something, Olive? I can't hear above the rain,' she asks, tilting her head sideways.

How far above the rain do my words need to travel for people to be able to hear them? Olive thinks. She tries to calculate.

I'm tired of speaking when no-one understands and tired of being spoken to. Too many people have talked at me today – and have talked too quickly and words have stacked up in my head like too many eggs in a nest, her thoughts continue.

Jostling for her attention is the number of people who've attended the funeral minus the number who haven't. Then there's the number of people who've driven there minus those who've taken the bus. Not to mention the number of friends present minus the handful of family members.

'Blah, blah, blah,' says a voice in her head because all this is exhausting. 'Nothing about my counting checks my fear, brings me comfort or stops my wondering why I couldn't save my father.'

Olive's nose begins to run and because she's concerned not to make a fool of herself and because her worst fear is of breaking down in public, she walks away from the graveside and stands at the back of the group.

The minister is still speaking although he began by saying, 'I'm no speaker'. He never met Frank and it is true that in his sermon he rather loses track of Frank whom he says is dead only to those who never met him.

'None of us can remain in the present because we live in time and time is constantly changing. Love may manifest itself - but only for a split second. The way to be happy is to go with the flow and enjoy the journey. Remember, man, that you are dust and to dust you will return...' A wave of assent goes through the group and Olive wonders why dust should make people react this way and if the minister is a nice person.

He is asking himself how he might bring in Proverbs 20.20 about honouring your parents or your lamp will be extinguished.

He wonders whether anyone will guess that 'lamps' have something to do with happiness.

His words continue to forge a cold, clammy path up Olive's skin. He speaks of happiness, but, for the moment, being happy is out of the question for her. All the weeping around her makes her feel uncomfortable and she can't understand – let alone put into words – that what she feels is rage.

'The minister can't possibly feel sorry for the death of someone he has never met, and I can't pretend to like him for that would be exhausting and rude. The thought that Frank might continue his life in a place I can't find or tread a path I can't follow is too painful to bear. And here I am listening to a sermon when all I really want to do is go home,' she says to no-one.

The sermon is over. The minister places a comforting hand on Olive's arm. 'I am sorry for your loss,' he says as if the death of a father in the year of one's thirty-second birthday were a normal occurrence.

She flinches.

I don't know why people never say what they mean, she thinks.

The service ends as a rainbow enters the sky like an actor taking centre stage. The rainbow stands there, round and bright while Rose and Olive cling to each other as if to keep a hold of each other and of Frank before he disappears along with the colours. The feel of Olive's body next to hers is one of the things Rose thinks about for weeks to come.

'You've all been kind and I haven't thanked you,' Rose calls out to the mourners, waving her flowered umbrella in the air, 'you must all come back for tea.'

She knows, of course, that everyone will stay around only long enough to offer condolences before going home to resume their own lives.

'Don't leave me – I can't put up with another leaving,' she turns to Olive after all the voices at the funeral have called out their goodbyes. She is caught between wanting Olive to come home again and wanting her to go back to her little wooden house and her smile hangs hopeful and small on her face.

Olive looks at her mother, a tired old woman with dyed blonde hair tucked under a straw hat standing in the middle of a graveyard.

My mother is still beautiful, she thinks, and has a hat for every occasion.

She would like nothing more than to continue to hold Rose against her chest as they face Frank's death together. Instead, she takes the umbrella out of her mother's hand and holds on to it as if on to a part of her body, then she drapes her shawl around Rose's shoulders. It is in this moment that she wonders if she has disappointed Rose who believes she can be anyone she wants to be whereas Olive can only be herself.

'I'll take you home now, Rose' she says.

Rose lets herself be led away because these are among the kindest words she has heard since Frank's passing.

I see the same angel in Olive I saw in Frank, she thinks, and she smiles at her daughter in the same way she might smile at a rose.

When she crosses her threshold that evening, Rose is alone. Her first step into her house marks the transition from having a husband to being on her own and from that moment on – and for a long time after that, nothing in her life seems to go right.

When Olive returns to her little wooden house, she spends some stoical time boiling an egg and eating it with a slice of toast and a banana while the story of Frank's funeral plays over and over in her head. However carefully she retells the story, however carefully she counts the hours, the people and events surrounding it, she can't help thinking that the ritual she was compelled to watch had nothing to do with him.

At least I didn't cry in public, she thinks.

The night of the funeral is warm and still and there are more stars in the sky than Olive can count. After spending hours sobbing into her pillow which becomes smudged with the Dusky Pink she borrowed from Rose, she plaits her hair, picks up her bag and wraps her green shawl twice around her neck. She has no clear plan except to leave her house. She locks her door behind her, takes off the wellington boots she has been wearing all day and carries them while she walks two thousand paces across the sand, hoping that walking will give her clues to her next move and leaving behind a trail of irregular footprints.

She finds herself at Frank's grave. She kneels and puts her hand on the mound of earth covering it, then presses her mouth in a kiss to the ground. She puts her legs into the earth. The wind blows salt in her face and the sounds of the distant waves echo through the sky. After the shock of damp on her feet, comes a sense of surprise that she's moving and breathing while her father lies still and lifeless below. She takes from her bag the wooden angel Frank carved and buries it as far down in the soil as she can reach. 'Cheers to life, Frank' she says, 'You can't beat life.'

She feels worn out. She extracts her legs from the soil, lies down and falls asleep under the deep dark sky, using her arm as a pillow.

When she wakes, her shawl is still wrapped around her neck, her boots are beside her and she is unaware at first that the sun – like a blessing –has risen to where it should be.

Frank brought me to him, she thinks. My experience during the night was as much his as mine.

Above her head a plover flies down like a messenger sent from another world and says in Frank's voice, 'things change like the tides and there's nothing you can do to stop them. You've had your yesterdays. You now need tomorrows.'

It then tilts its head, spreads its wings and catches the wind.

Olive covers her face with her shawl and cries as unobtrusively as she can manage before standing up and dragging her foot the long way home.

When Rose hears about Olive's night in the cemetery, she says, 'I don't understand why Olive does what she does. I don't understand things.'

She does add, though, 'While I might not be able to understand things here on earth, I am sure that everything is working to plan. This has to be so.'

Her main concern for now is how to continue to be a good friend to someone who is no longer there to say what he expects.

'No-one will miss me if I die,' Olive tells her. She says this without self-pity. It is just her opinion.

2002

Her story is common enough, but the year of the two deaths feels to Rose like it belongs to someone else. At first, she can't stop herself expecting to see Frank around every corner. She imagines that he's merely obscured from her vision and that she'll go into his workshop to find she hasn't been able to see him simply because she has forgotten to switch on the light. And things keep coming up which made her think, I must go and tell Frank.

These imaginings are soon replaced by a dull ache which won't go away and which is all the more painful because Rose is not one of those people who air wrongs or ask for sympathy or whose mourning is 'significant' in any way.

For three whole weeks she goes to bed and buries her head in the same pillow on which her happy hair once spread out like sunbeams and she stays like that crying and thinking that her story is at an end.

She doesn't dress herself or do her hair. She dreams that she is lying on a bed of rose petals she has watered with her tears, not knowing where the petals stop and she begins. Some of her nights are so wakeful that she is glad to see that when the sun comes up – shy of entering her house and eavesdropping on her grief, everything in her bedroom is where it should be.

There are days when she stares into the mirror for so long that hundreds of Roses appear to be staring back at her. She looks at her wallpaper. If she looks one way she sees trellises. If she looks another, she sees the roses which are climbing all over them and she begins to wonder how the roses on her wallpaper grow so luxuriously when the roses in her garden seem to have lost their spirit and become dreary.

When asked how she is, she answers, 'I am fine, I am fine' and she emphasise the 'fine'. 'We – Olive and I, that is, are living our own lives. No-one knows how experiences deserve to be told, but, after Frank, all I do is wander into places where he is not. The truth is, I have no idea how to live without him.'

If she leaves her bed at all, it is to flick her duster here and there to deal with the worst of the dust or to walk around aimlessly – in and out of the kitchen, in and out of the bedrooms, into the living room to sit on Edith's rocking chair and check the time.

'I wanted to be a woman standing in sunshine and didn't ask for any of this,' she tells Olive. 'All I remember of the week of the two funerals is that the sky was ablaze with the colours of the rainbow and all I've done ever since is spend whole days staring into space.'

In some ways Olive feels she has died, too. She tries not to think of Frank because no amount of thinking will bring him back, but she has put his death away in a quiet place with a plan to take it out later and consider it.

'I enjoy staring into space up to a point, but not for whole days,' she replies.

Months slip by unnoticed, but time scoops up mother and daughter and pushes them on. One August day about a year later, Rose abandons grief when she realises that she hasn't bothered with it for a while.

She looks around and heaves a deep sigh. She has slept through a season and missed the first snow on the town for ten years. The house is a mess and she has lost weight.

At least a spring of rain has washed life into my roses, she thinks.

'Death is life – as final as can be, but there is a limit to everything,' Rose announces, 'it's as simple as that. Everything must end at some point and one death, one day, will be mine. There is even a chance I'll meet Frank in an afterlife and share cake with him for the rest of time.'

In so saying, she feels she has deciphered something of the mystery of the universe right there in her bedroom where roses climb up trellises and birds lay eggs in nests all over the wallpaper.

As if a magical decree from heaven changed sadness into action, she takes most of Frank's clothes to a charity shop.

'You can't beat life,' she tells the owner of the shop.

She bundles his cap and shoes into an old pillowcase which she discards and folds his overcoat into a ball which she gives to Olive. In the emptiness of Frank's absence, she washes salt out of her sea-green curtains and sweeps away handfuls of cobwebs.

One tea-time, the sun which has tired of her grief, slips into the house and stays longer than usual, brightening the furniture and lighting up the walls.

'Hello old friend,' says Rose.

Although the figure of Frank never leaves the threshold of her awareness, she begins to sing along to the radio – albeit tentatively - and bakes her first cake even if she needs to measure everything twice. She spends days bent over her roses till her back resembles a comma.

'To stay put in this house without your father is to see him everywhere - but what kind of wife would I be if I moved or abandoned him from my thinking simply because he was dead?' she asks Olive on an afternoon when Olive is wrapped up in her green shawl busy taping Frank's tools into boxes.

'Something is the matter. What's the matter?' she asks Rose with features so apparently devoid of expression, she resembles a plate.

'Two hammers, three chisels, four screwdrivers, one lathe – into the box.' On and on Olive goes, counting and cutting tape with her teeth.

Rose decides that her first excursion should be to the library to see Mr Gorkin, the librarian, who worked with her mother before she retired. She wonders whether Edith spoke to him of Frank or of her father and is full of tingling to know his answers.

On a day when the sun shines brightly, she arrives at the library with a cake. 'I've brought you a cake, Mr Gorkin,' she says, 'baked with marrows from the garden.' As no cake has tasted quite the same since Frank's passing, she adds, 'although the missing ingredient might be Frank.'

Mr Gorkin is a bachelor who looks different from most other people in the town. Rose can't know how he has changed – how he has learned to fend for himself. She does know that he seldom leaves his house and that when he does, he wears a raincoat whether in rain or shine.

Mr Gorkin tells whoever cares to listen that he lives in a place where not to be a Jew is desirable and that although he can see forests and fields if he drives a mile or two from his house, he feels he has no business with them nor they with him.

When he sees Rose in the library, he decides to express his sympathy for her by sharing his own stories.

Although, I am never exactly sure what people want or do not want to hear, he thinks.

With his gaze held firmly on the bookshelves behind her, he says, 'I am sorry for your loss. Everyone needs to make sense of their losses. I myself long for a time which can never be repeated. I lost my parents somewhere between my fifth and sixth birthdays and only one sister remains to speak of them. Although I like to think of them enjoying their lives in heaven, their story is in a book someone needs to write before Jews become a meaningless part of the earth and no-one is Jewish anymore. Have you heard of Hitler?'

Rose smiles at the floor.

She thinks of her own father. For all she knows, he may have liberated the camps and returned from the war a different man – a man unable to face her mother. For all she knows. She allows herself a moment to wonder why he never wrote and, more fancifully, to wonder whether he might have been Jewish.

What is it about fathers? she thinks, Olive lost hers, too.

She lights a cigarette, puts it down on a saucer and peels back the foil covering her marrow cake on the pretext of inspecting it while deciding how to reply.

'I sometimes find it hard to know what to say,' she begins, 'while I've put mourning behind me, I've not really been the same since. All I can tell you is that any people I have lost haven't become meaningless parts of the earth because they remain in my head and my heart. I, too, am trying to find meaning in life's messiness,' and she points around her to try to indicate the extent of the 'messiness'.

She is moved by his story and by the fact that he comes from a country she doesn't know and she's afraid to keep talking lest her chat offend him or seem like a desecration of past suffering.

She always suspected that people preferred Frank to her and that she might not be liked as much because she lacks strong opinions on the town or the sea or people and because she doesn't dwell on the meaning of this or that.

Frank made every day mean something, she thinks.

'I find meaning in prayer. I believe in prayer,' Mr Gorkin says, appearing to read her mind and stepping out of the way of the stream of smoke rising from her cigarette as if she weren't standing in front of him.

Rose is trying to believe in God and heaven. 'I love anything spiritual,' she says, tilting her head to the side.

When he doesn't reply she adds, 'what an interesting life you've had.'

She finds a knife and cuts into her cake.

'What do you pray for?' she asks, offering him a slice.

'Good question,' he replies.

'I don't know what I was thinking when I asked,' she says and blushes.

Then she walks out of the library with a book with hydrangeas on the cover she doesn't need, and that seems to put an end to that.

3
2003

Frank has been dead for two years and his part is over.

Rose is seventy-four now and while she goes back to living as she did before Frank died, time has changed her like flowing water must re-shape the earth. She has the strangest feeling that she's taking his place in the world and she is sure she is noticing things about people she didn't before.

He may as well be alive and watching me from the sky, I picture him so clearly, she thinks, but did I do my best by him?

'Olive and I – we – are not doing too badly,' she tells the Frank in the sky, 'better than you could have imagined. Olive walks as she did when you were alive and the scent of roses fills the house as it did when you were here. I wish I had known about the trouble you had with your heart. I often think I could have prevented your dying.'

She hopes he is listening from wherever in the sky his soul has settled.

On a day when the sea's flat and shiny, and Frank's presence strong, Rose scrapes together her courage and invites Mr Gorkin to her husbandless house for tea.

She wakes early, bakes a cake and spends the rest of the morning in the garden. When she realises how long she has stayed out there, she leaves her spade planted in the earth and goes inside to place marzipan roses on her cake. She then packs roses into vases till all her rooms smell of marzipan and roses.

Roses aren't decorative for nothing, she thinks, eyeing the vases and the marzipan roses before going upstairs to change into a pink dress covered with green roses.

Mr Gorkin arrives as the clock strikes three.

He has a long nervous face which looks as if it has seen better days. His eyebrows are joined together and bounce up and down when he talks as if to emphasise his opinions. His accent's that of a man who belongs in no particular country and he retains a faded courtesy left over, perhaps, from his childhood. He is five years younger than Rose and energetic for his age but his work in the library has made him silent and his manner is so discreet, he is almost invisible. He lives in the only unpainted house in his street and its interior remains unchanged since the 1950s except for the addition of a microwave cooker and a computer. No-one knows why there's a row of old sewing machines wedged to the top of his garden wall.

When he walks towards Rose with his small steps, she imagines, for a moment, that he is Frank grown old and that she has dreamed Frank's death, but she checks herself and calls out his name without turning around.

'How do you know it's me?' he asks.

'By your walk,' she replies, 'but don't creep up on me again. You made me jump.'

'I live in the same town as you and have never seen your roses,' he says.

Rose doesn't like to mention that she has passed his house but not seen inside it and that she feels more comfortable, anyway, visiting him in the library. She also doesn't say that she thought he was Frank and that the only reason she decided he wasn't, was because he isn't wearing Frank's clothes.

They sit down to tea.

'Your marrow cake is so good it tastes like praying,' he says. He wipes icing off his chin, raises a hand and bows to the cake.

'Thank you. Frank loved it,' she replies, holding her head to one side – not something she did with Frank when she stared straight into his mismatched eyes. She shakes crumbs from her napkin on to the grass so the birds can eat them and none go to waste.

'That bird is singing in D minor,' he says.

'Your hair is really brown,' she replies.

'Everyone in my family had brown hair,' he says and his eyebrows bounce. 'They all had brown hair, and, although I am not someone who sees himself as having had parents, particularly because memory is imprecise after all, as far as I can be sure, their hair never turned grey.'

He laughs but his laugh is less an expression of mirth than an indication that there's no more to be said on the subject.

Rose joins in the laughter as if a private joke were being shared. The image of her own dyed blonde hair crosses her mind. No female member of her family ever seemed satisfied with the hair colour their parents gifted. Edith had begun to dye her hair blue before she died, for God's sake.

'While I can find nothing to say about my parents, I do know something about longing and belonging,' he continues. 'When the war ended, I had to redefine myself from being a part of something to being alone except for one sister and I have not returned to the country of my birth. I only hope my parents had a happy marriage and are buried near each other. I am not in favour of death.'

And this he says while clematis are dying up and down his garden wall, she thinks.

'I have often wondered if my father was Jewish,' she says. Her thoughts are skipping about delighting in their existence. I am behaving like a woman I don't know, she thinks.

'I once heard the voice of God – or it might have been the sound of my soul but I've struggled to hear it since,' he muses.

'Cheers to life,' she says and agrees with him – whatever he means. She has not heard anyone speak like this before and is enjoying herself especially as she imagined they would spend their time talking about her cakes.

She begins to scatter around phrases like 'least said soonest mended' and 'seize the day' and 'still waters run deep' and she licks her lips as if to taste her words.

Mr Gorkin is enjoying the conversation as much as she is but says 'it does not do to be talking too much about life – the good and the bad of it.'

They plan to meet again as Rose is a planner – it is one of her many personalities – and she plans what she is going to say next.

On a hot afternoon when Rose thinks she can smell the green melting off the leaves of her roses, they plan to drive to the beach.

Mr Gorkin is wearing a suit and blue shirt which matches his socks and carrying his raincoat. He creeps into her house after wiping his feet up and down the doormat and raises his trilby.

Rose tries and fails to say something more interesting than 'this is the best summer's day ever.'

They plan to drive in his worn and slightly elderly maroon Ford Fiesta he has spent the morning polishing and he parks it in Rose's driveway where it gleams in the sun. Frank taught Rose to drive, and she drives, but doesn't enjoy it and prefers being driven. It is such a simple way to be taken from the familiar to the unfamiliar, she thinks.

Mr Gorkin opens the car door. The car is so full of books and papers, she might be forgiven for thinking he lived in it if she didn't know better. She looks at her watch, 'I am ready,' she says but doesn't know for what.

He begins by asking if she is fine with the route he is taking then he presses down on the accelerator and they proceed slowly and carefully along a road which leads to the sea and Olive's house.

On the back seat of the car is a bunch of roses. She wonders if it's a present for her then she settles back to watch as they move away from her street to a part of the town where shops and rows of coloured houses are replaced by gorse and mounds of sand.

Rose is wearing a silk dress and pearl necklace under a beaded cardigan. She has on her wellington boots over her shoes - for the sand -and has taken along both her flowered umbrella and a straw hat because she loves hats. On her lap is a tartan bag filled with food.

With Frank gone, she is no longer sure how to dress; if she dresses up, she might look too eager, but she can't wear any old clothes.

Mr Gorkin considers Rose's presence to be something of a miracle and thinks she looks like an exotic bird which has dropped out of its nest.

'Will you be more comfortable if you take off your boots?' he suggests.

She smiles.

There is no air conditioning in the car, and they continue their journey with all the windows down. Rose pulls the lever to incline her seat back and tilts her face to the sun which dazzles on to the dashboard. She closes her eyes and thinks about the peculiarity of riding in a car with a man who isn't her husband. Memories of Frank with his eyes on her face and hands around hers come flooding in like so many mice escaping the traps she lays in the kitchen. Rose wants not to think of him. She tries, instead, to think about Edith whose husband's legacy was the clothes he left in his wardrobe and who had to spend most of her life dealing with neighbours' gossip and worse, their pity. Rose goes from feeling special to wondering if she can ever be sure she is doing the right thing.

'I wish I could reach back my arm and rearrange time,' she says.

It is his turn to smile.

Just then the sea comes into sight and there is Olive passing them on her way home from a night's walking. They swerve around her, but she doesn't see them.

'Olive lives in a different world from the rest of us,' Rose says. She would like to talk about Olive but how to explain children to someone who has none?

They sit in silence.

'Love is all you need – as I think the Beatles sang,' he says inexplicably – and to break the silence.

'That's a point of view,' says Rose, gathering her tartan bag to her then pushing her sunglasses up her nose.

Why did I say point of view? she thinks. She fears she might start prattling – saying anything that comes into her head and only afterwards wondering, is that the kind of person I am?

When they reach the sea, the car judders to a halt as if it has decided to do so. Mr Gorkin takes the tartan bag and gives Rose his arm.

'Here we are,' he says, glancing at her because she appears to be rearranging her thoughts.

They head to the beach at the base of the rocks on which Olive's house perches and sit on cushions he has brought along.

Rose keeps her knees together and her tartan bag close.She has packed enough food to sustain them for days and this lifts her spirit. They share bread and butter, boiled eggs, apples, chicken legs and marrow cake. She lights a cigarette and Frank's face smiles at her from behind the twisted smoke.

'Will you call me Alfred?' he asks.

'More marrow cake, Alfred?' she asks.

He removes his trilby, wipes the sweat off his forehead with a handkerchief then replaces it.

'Your food is so good it will be the death of me,' he says.

Rose agrees with him as if she had the same thought herself.

'You are very kind,' she says, but she is thinking of Frank. She holds out her hands as if to push all thinking away.

'Life is an awfully funny thing,' he suggests because he doesn't know how else to respond to her compliment.

'I have been thinking about life,' says Rose. 'You can say all sorts of things about it, but it doesn't make what you say real. I, for one, see angels everywhere. Frank is an angel. What do you think of angels, by the way?'

Her question rolls its way along the sand and into the sea.

Together, they sit with their backs to the rocks and watch gulls flying over the water. A boat sails past, then another. The sun sends out golden sequins of light and everything around them shines with an almost biblical radiance. Something about the shimmers of sun on water makes Rose feel sad. The movement of the waves – the sea receding from view – make her feel that something in her life is receding too – her strength, perhaps, or her feeling of connectedness to things. It might even be her past which, at this moment, seems so distant that Rose wonders if she should concern herself more with what should have happened than with what did happen and whether anyone would care. She clutches on to her tartan bag.

She peeps at Alfred who is so silent and lost in thought, she keeps from talking lest she interrupt him because, for all she knows, he is praying. And it is at this point on this perfectly ordinary day that his goodness is all too much for her and it is all she can do to stop herself running across the sand and jumping into the sea.

She can't help feeling connected to Frank. She has never known anyone as strong as Frank and if she found his strength too much to bear it was because she didn't know what she has come to learn: that so much of life is shaped by an absence of gratitude – so much of life is wasted.

I wish I had paid more attention to Frank, she thinks.

She claps her hands. 'Let's get back,' she says, 'the sun is beginning to set.'

She never stays anywhere long. She is always half-way to leaving or half-way to arriving.

'Things might be better now – without the sun's glare,' he suggests, 'or shall we finish our picnic in the car?'

'I'm not that fond of the sun,' she lies, tilting her head to the side as cheerily as she can because she feels inexplicably exposed – then adds 'or of cars.'

The setting sun continues to shine gold across the water and on to Olive who is sitting on the rocks above them imagining that if Frank's soul settles anywhere, it will be near the sea.

Neither Rose nor Alfred says anything as they pack the remaining food into the tartan bag. What is there to say? she thinks.

Life is life. Why complicate it? he thinks.

Rose remembers her roses. She knows about them and loves them and is most herself among them and not here by the sea.

'I must get back to my roses,' she says, 'I often garden in moonlight even if I struggle to make out what needs doing.' She wants to smile but can't manage it and fears that if she stays away any longer, her roses will just give up on her and die.

'What is it like to spend your life among flowers?' he asks.

The sky prepares for night.

They drive away and when they reach Rose's house, he smiles. She smiles. He looks younger when he smiles, she thinks.

She stays in the car with her hand on her tartan bag before getting out and walking up her narrow driveway between the rows of roses which look phosphorescent in the moonlight. She's glad to see they can continue blooming whether she is there or not.

'Goodnight,' she calls out.

'Goodnight,' he replies, watching her beaded cardigan glint up the garden path. Then he sits in his car and stares at her house for what feels like an age because he doesn't know what else to do.

I don't understand her, he thinks, but then most people are a whole bunch of selves. All I have to offer are stories of things I gave up or never began – she must have trouble understanding me, too.

Rose senses his eyes on her back as she puts her key in the lock. When she is inside her house, she looks at her wristwatch and it's nine o'clock. So much time has passed, she thinks. She doesn't bother to turn on the lights but goes straight up to bed and gives thanks that she has a place to come back to, that no-one she knows has been in a concentration camp and that she has never needed to pack a bag and run off into the night.

In another version of the day's events she might have told Alfred about her life with Frank and about Olive's leaving. She might have spoken about Olive's limp and her solitude and her little wooden house. But she did not.

She stands at her window and watches him from behind her sea-green curtains till his car is swallowed by the dark.

In time, everything about this day will become shrouded in mist and when she comes to turn it over in her memory, she will find – as she usually does – that it will be easier to substitute the conversation she should have had for the one she had.

'In its way, it should have been an acceptable day, but it was not,' she tells the Frank in the sky, 'he either forgot to give me the bunch of roses on the back seat of his car or he changed his mind.' Then her hanging lamp with the parchment shade goes from dark to light and back to dark again.

Still seated in his car and still in her driveway, Alfred is seized by an immense and sudden weariness. One can think too much, he thinks.

He places his raincoat on the seat beside him, puts his trilby on top of it and laughs for no good reason - at a private joke, perhaps. His laughter is sad and happy – sad because Rose slipped out of his grasp – like desire – and happy because no-one could deny that at one point, he knew her.

With his head propped against the driver's seat headrest, he falls asleep and dreams that he goes to every house in the town asking if anyone knows his family. He drives away when dawn breaks.

Rose doesn't hear him leave. She is in her bed.

When she wakes, she creeps out to her rose bushes where slugs have made holes in the leaves, just to make sure the green hasn't melted off them entirely.

4

2003

Olive is thirty-four and works in a supermarket where she feeds her love of numbers in a moderate way but her life centres around sea and sky and she continues to walk around the town as if she owned it.

Her best walking takes place in the dark when she takes herself away from the pity and funny notions people get in their heads during the daytime. She walks, torch in hand, past sleeping houses and people and directs her light at the night creatures she comes across– owls, bats and stray dogs. Sometimes, she lifts insects from the ground to inspect them before releasing them back to their homes and their lives. When she returns to her own home, she imagines the sea to be a giant resting beneath her and its smells and sounds soothe her. On summer nights when it is too hot to settle, she takes out a sheet on to a rock she has made her own and lets the cool feel of stone send her to sleep.

Let her be grown up, Rose prays – and then Olive is. What needs to change, changes. Life resumes its uncertain course and she grows up despite the doubts of the townspeople and watched closely by them because living in a small town is like living in a glasshouse.

The period since Frank's passing has been empty and silent for her. She doesn't understand what was wrong with him. Had he told her, she would have asked him to do something.

'Doctors can do things,' is what she would have said.

Frank started building her house long before she decided to make it her own. She had barely looked around before saying she would like to move in as soon as possible and now she can't afford to live alone any other way.

Her house isn't much of a house – more a hut – and its position near rocks makes it look like a strange spaceship about to take off. All sorts of creatures wander in and out of it; toads take up residence outside the front door, moths and dragonflies brush her arms and bats return each summer to breed. Two owls with large golden eyes once stared at Olive from within touching distance.

It's a short walk to the beach and her house's proximity to the sea represents for Olive one of those strokes of luck which occur only once or twice in a lifetime.

'I can no more leave my house by the sea than leave my own skin and death alone will part me from it because everybody has to die someday,' she tells Rose, 'or else the sea might wash everything away.'

She has furnished it in an unplanned way and it smells of sea and sunshine in summer and wood from a wood burning stove in winter. Frank's coat hangs on a hook and on dark days it looks as if he himself is hanging there, slouched against the wall. There is one sofa in a corner which doubles as a bed and is strategically placed so that when she sits on it, she can see the sea. A wooden chest sits next to it and she has arranged various dolls, boats, shells, driftwood, dried seaweed, feathers and pebbles on a low shelf. She doesn't own a television set or computer and has a mirror but no wardrobe. Her clothes sit in piles in a corner, smelling of moist salt and musty wood.

When she stands before her mirror she sees the rather serious, physically awkward woman who inherited Frank's stubbornness but none of her mother's fragility. Although her smile is beautiful and her skin glows, she thinks of herself as unattractive and continues to wear mostly green; her shawls are green and the apron she cooks in is green. While she knows which mushrooms are poisonous and which are not and can recite almost all the street names in the town, she still feels like a child.

In the stillness of the night when the sky is black and she wraps her duvet around her, Olive dreams of love. Although the dreams are vague, in them she is always nestling in a man's arms – a strong man with strong hands who lives in the town.

Olive accepts Rose's infrequent visits. She doesn't want Rose's pity. When Rose does arrive – cake in hand – they usually walk together to the beach where Olive swims or watches dogs bark and splash and Rose shakes sand off her dress and shoes and says, 'this is the best summer's day ever.' Rose's aversion to the sea and everything about it confuses Olive and when she asks her mother how she came to be her daughter, Rose tuts and assures her of her love.

On a crowded day when it is so hot people are sitting in the sea rather than on the sand, Rose joins Olive – cake in hand. Olive doesn't like sitting in the sun as much as her mother does and has spent the morning dipping in and out of the waves.

'It's the kind of day which makes me want to be alone with the sea,' she tells Rose.

Rose says, 'I always know where to find you' and sits down on the 'safe' sand-proof plastic rug she has brought along with her.

Although Rose fears the sea, she can't prevent Olive from swimming out further than she would like even though she knows Olive is a strong swimmer and even though Olive assures her there is nothing to fear out to sea but seagulls. Rose's idea of being in the water is to wander about at the edge of it and she wonders if Olive swims to drown out the memory of Frank.

There is a blue mist over the waves and Rose searches anxiously every time Olive goes into them; she watches her being swept and down and holds her breath every time her daughter disappears.

When Olive swims, she always imagines that the whole of the sea is washing into her; she feels alone and significant when she swims. She swims so much her hair is turning green. She often swims at night after walking not thinking – as Rose does – that if anything were to happen to her, no-one would know.

The sun soothes Rose to sleep and when she wakes, Olive is crouched beside her, arranging shells in piles. Rose tries to push away the sun's brightness by stretching out her hands.

'Isn't it hot?' she says, 'at least the sea is bigger than daily life.'

I wonder what I mean by that, she thinks.

On this, the hottest day, she has brought along her floral umbrella – 'because you never know' – and it sits in her tartan bag along with foil wrapped sandwiches.

'Egg and cress or chicken and mustard, Olive?' she offers.

Olive looks at the parcels and says, 'no thanks. Will you come into the water?'

'I'd rather stay in the sun,' answers Rose, who has something to say.

She puts on her sunglasses.

Olive puts hers on as well.

Rose asks if she can smoke on the beach then lights a cigarette and blows smoke into the air. She shuts her eyes and says – as casually as possible, 'I have something to say.'

For a moment she feels the waves might be stopping midway towards the shore.

Olive glances at her suspiciously.

'Do you ever wonder what keeps people going?' Rose begins, 'for example, do you remember Alfred Gorkin?'

'The Jewish man?' asks Olive who feels tight and apprehensive suddenly and who can't think of anything else to say.

'Will you please not call him "the Jewish man",' says Rose. 'Alfred and I spent time together and I felt I might be able to marry – just fall in love once more – if only for a short while but I have decided not to see him again. There is always a struggle between what to do and what not to do and you never know how these things will turn out. You think you do, but you don't?' She finishes with an interrogatory rise of voice and speaks with the seriousness of someone announcing a death or a war. She inhales again. There's so little of which she is sure.

She looks at Olive whose potential unhappiness always makes her nervous. She fears she might be making her unhappy just at this moment when this is the last thing in the world she wants to do.

'I shouldn't burden you with this?' she continues

Olive can't abide the smell of cigarette smoke and it makes no difference to her that Rose smokes only occasionally or that she has cut back to two a day. Olive has never smoked.

When Rose turns towards her, she looks away and asks, 'do you know that cigarettes can kill you?'

'I've never heard that before,' laughs Rose.

The truth is that Rose feels she has lived long enough for her smoking not to be a problem and, anyway, she has heard that smoking is good for loneliness. She frets more about the tides.

'They change every day,' Olive assures her but she isn't assured.

'You don't want to see Alfred again?' she asks – just to be sure.

'I don't suppose I do,' Rose replies.

Rose has made her life with Frank sound like a fairy tale filled with roses and marrows and in all the time Rose has known Alfred, Olive has been terrified lest her mother fall for someone who isn't Frank and rub out the years the three of them spent together.

I'll never match the love Rose and Frank felt for one another, she thinks.

'Did you love Alfred?, she asks and her eyes move from Rose's face to somewhere behind her head.

Rose stretches out her arms and pushes away the air. 'I'm not sure love can do anything for me – after Frank,' she says, 'I'm not sure love is as special as people say? It might be, but what do I know?' She throws her cigarette in the direction of a bin behind her and wonders if Olive has noticed.

'The truth is no-one knows anything about love?' she continues. Her voice rises again with the uncertainty of her position and her words pass like rainclouds over Olive's head.

The two women sit in silence. There were hardly any birds to be seen in the hot middle of the day – only dragonflies and mosquitoes – but as the afternoon wears on, birds of all sizes begin to swoop down to stab fish and fly off with them in their beaks.

'I'm going to lie in the sand, and I might just wait until the tide comes in and washes me away,' says Olive who fears Rose might continue talking – and talking cheerily.

'Washes you away?' Rose asks. The sun has warmed her back like an old cardigan but she doesn't like the beach as much as she likes the road leading from it to her house.

You never know with beaches, she thinks.

She searches around for her keys in her tartan bag.

'Time I went. I'm tired,' she says.

'Same here,' says Olive.

'Look after yourself,' says Rose, struggling to her feet. She looks at her wristwatch and can't hold back from adding, 'I'm tired of the sea.'

The day has been difficult for her. She walks off and waves but doesn't look back for fear that if she does, Olive might disappear or with all that swimming – you never know - turn into a pillar of salt.

She steps along the sand towards the car park, holding her tartan bag in one hand and steadying her hat with the other and looking like a woman on the verge of falling.

Olive sees her grow smaller and smaller till she disappears altogether just as if she had waded fully clothed into the sea with her blonde hair immaculate under her hat.

Rose walks twice around the car park till she finds her car which receives her like a hug. She sits down at the driver's seat with her legs hanging outside and knocks the sand out of her shoes then she swings her legs back inside, closes the door and drives home.

I held out on the beach longer than planned, she thinks, and all I want now is to see my roses before the night turns them black.

Olive waits to see if Rose will turn back but she doesn't so she sits without moving and looks at the sea which speaks to her like the friend it is. She buries her feet and lets the hot sand run through her toes. Did the afternoon happen? she wonders.

When the last car has left the car park and the afternoon changes softly into night, she can step on the sand without burning her feet. She takes off all her clothes and with a splash and a gasp wades into the sea.

She turns on to her back and floats and the sea tickles her, sprays salt into her mouth and soothes her soul. She feels light. She looks up at the moon which is whole and exposed, and she swims further and deeper till the seaweed which fills the sea wraps itself around her thighs and Rose is of less concern to her than the water's icy touch.

She returns to the beach when she is pink and shiny, her skin puckered and tasting of salt and the sky is blushed with dawn. She kneels in the sand for a long while before being able to stand because she feels so weak.

The following day passes then another, then another, and with each day which passes, unexplained anger swells up inside her. Olive has never known what to do with anger, so she does nothing until it continues to grow and move through her body like a rosebush ready to spike and she can no longer contain it.

Why am I waiting? she thinks.

She says goodbye to her photograph and sets off for the library. She knows most of the streets in the town like the palm of her hand and when she leaves her house and keeps on walking, her legs usually drag her to where she wants to go. All roads lead back to the ocean, anyway, she thinks. If she doesn't know an exact route, she walks with the feeling of Frank's arm around her shoulders and the chance of getting lost doesn't frighten her.

Soon she finds herself standing outside the library next to the maroon Ford Fiesta without a clear idea of how she came there, why she made the journey or what sheis about to say. If she left her house with a plan, it all went downhill on her journey when every step she took became a question and she begins to realise she has left her plan by the sea.

She moves to the window and presses her palms against the glass.

A strange intuition prompted Alfred to stay in the library later than usual. He is lost in a daydream and is sitting at his desk with his spectacles pushed up his forehead.

'Today is a day I need to spend time in silence beneath a lamp which is not my own,' he says to a moth circling the light which is making him look like he is glowing from within.

When he hears a sound he thinks is a bird pecking on glass, he waves his hands as if to brush bad thoughts away, stops what he is doing and looks out of the window.

What shadow is chasing me? he wonders.

He sees Olive tapping for his attention.

He wonders how long she has been there and asks himself, at first, who she is. Then, as recognition arrives gradually – like nightfall, he knows – and in the moments between not knowing and knowing, he feels out of control and as if he is falling through water which is a frightening feeling because he can't swim.

Does she want something? is his first thought because his time in the library has taught him that everyone is searching for something. His second thought is, is she sad? – but then, whoever knows about somebody else's sadness?

What in God's name are you doing here? he wants to ask but because the two of them have previously not exchanged more than hellos and goodbyes, he decides not to say too much.

I said too much to Rose and look where that got me, he thinks.

Olive has no make-up on, as usual, but on her wrist are various shell bracelets she has made. She is wearing green trousers she could have sewn herself and a yellow blouse with red roses printed on it which is made of a synthetic material which makes her sweat. Although it is hot enough for her green trousers to stick to her legs, she still has her green shawl draped over her shoulders. She works to flap her trousers free from her thighs and dabs her damp forehead with her shawl.

Since Frank's death, she has coiled up her hair into a bun, but a breeze arrives with the evening and blows her hair around in all directions like an unruly halo. She runs her fingers through her unkempt strands in an attempt to tame them.

He must imagine I don't own a comb, she thinks.

Olive wants to meet the man her mother called a friend. She wants him to know about Rose and Frank, about the wooden house which Frank built, about her beach and her cat which will be going hungry and missing her by now and about Frank's dying over his steering wheel. She wants to ask him if he ever wonders what dying might be like and whether he thinks it might be like falling asleep. She wants to know if she can be sure death will happen to her. She wants to ask him about all this and about other things besides. She wants him to know about the difficulties of being the person who confuses people and from whom they drift away. She wants him to know that she left her home with anger, but that it has inexplicably turned itself off inside her – like a switch.

She feels the approaching storm in her stomach long before the rain falls but doesn't see the sky grow dull and the clouds turn thick and smoke grey. Before she knows it, water is splashing all over her shoes and hair and running like tears off the roses on her blouse.

Alfred stands up, goes to the door and steps aside to let Olive in.

'Is that you, Olive? Why are you here?' he asks not wanting to think about the strangeness of her wearing a damp shawl. 'Come in from the rain. Tea?' he suggests.

'Yes,' answers Olive, who doesn't drink tea. She wants to ask him why heis offering her tea, but this would be rude.

'Actually, it is not tea I want,' she says.

'What is it then?' he asks.

'I don't know,' she replies because she doesn't know. She started out with brave words, but her words have faded like dried rose petals in the sun.

He stirs two sugars slowly into his cup, sips his black tea and looks at her. She is young, he thinks and doesn't understand the effort it takes an old man to get up and walk to the kettle without falling over. He thinks this before realising how much effort she must make before taking any steps at all; it's as if her left leg always needs a moment longer than her right.

'I am sorry,' he says more to himself than to her. He spends so much of his life trying not to make mistakes – his English is that of a man who listens to the radio in order not to make mistakes.

Olive puts her shawl on the floor because the weight of it has become a burden. She sits beside him and pictures herself drinking tea. They remain together united, as they are, in a most unexpected way and without talking about what matters – if anything matters, he thinks. He is afraid to speak because his conversation might be the wrong conversation and he might be the wrong man.

If I speak, I'll cry, thinks Olive.

They keep silent until the silence in the room is so immense it feels as if all the silences they have ever known have gathered in the library to form a great silence as deep as the sea.

He wants to put his arms around her but fears this will turn her away so he holds out his arms towards her till he can hold them out no longer then he lowers them.

People think they know the mystery of living in your skin. They don't, he thinks.

'Here we are,' he says.

Olive glances at him. His eyes stare out from under his eyebrow and his thinning hair is pulled over his scalp. He is the most tired looking man she has ever met. She averts her gaze in a gesture of respect. She often sees through people's eyes into their souls and if she finds a story of fear or pain there, she can't concentrate on what she, herself, must do or say.

She had a story to tell – however small – and she isn't sure how to say now that part of what she came to share was that her life was once full of the goodness of Frank and that now he is gone. Her words stop inside her because she usually leaves the business of talking about feelings to other people.

Olive and Alfred share moments of silence – that is all, but everything from her trousers to her shirt feels tight and she needs to do something because it is a most unpleasant feeling.

I look terrible with my wet hair falling in strands over my face and my trousers stuck to my legs, she thinks, and all this despite the best efforts of the roses on my blouse to be happy and bright.

She hugs her knees and her shell bracelets tinkle as she looks at the thousands of books stacked all around her, so she doesn't have to look him in the eye.

'Why did you choose to work in a library?' she whispers because she hates libraries as much as he loves them.

She doesn't know why she whispers or why she asks. It sometimes happens that her words take her by surprise.

The ordinariness of her question puzzles Alfred and he wonders if Olive is mocking him.

This is unusual, he thinks.

'Books are my friends,' he replies and nearly adds, 'the compulsion to work is strong.'

He had hoped to write the story which needed to be written before Jews became a meaningless part of the earth, but it is now too late.

'I don't know much about anything except books,' he continues, 'I should also say that the library was the only place which would have me. Do you have any ideas about your future?'

'None,' says Olive, who smells peppermint on his breath.

'Someday you will,' he replies.

She lets this idea find a place in her mind.

'What happened to your father?' he asks because he wants to know.

His words feel like a wound, but Olive replies, 'my father is dead.'

'Mine too,' he says, 'not having a father is something we share.'

'I didn't expect him to die,' says Olive who has waited a long time to say this. She lives in a waiting state – this is what she does. She closes her eyes and thinks of Frank's gift to her – her house by the sea.

'You have Rose. She is your mother. She is you. You are her,' he replies.

'I must go now,' she says because she can't stay in this conversation much longer.

'What are your plans for this evening?' he asks, 'what are you going to do?'

'I'll be fine,' she says.

She has been in the library for no more than twenty minutes. Like Rose, she is always arriving or leaving, seldom staying.

'Do you need me to walk with you?' he asks.

'I'll find my own way, thank you,' she says and turns towards the door.

'It was nothing, nothing at all,' he assures her then continues, 'you should go home now because the rain has stopped. Only it hasn't,' he says looking at a rainbow which is shining its watery light over the world and as if the only reason Olive came into the library was to shelter from the rain. 'A rainbow is an answer, by the way – whatever the prayer.'

Does he know I collect rainbows? she wonders.

What to make of Olive's behaviour? he asks himself, had she planned to place all her hopes on a stranger, expecting that whatever he did or said would be just what she needed?

He holds out his hand and Olive looks at it as at something unfamiliar before taking it up in her own.

She smoothes out the creases in her trousers and sets off from the library's gloomy quiet for her world of familiar sounds like lapping tides and seabirds' cries.

He calls to her retreating back, 'believe in something whether it is God or other people or yourself. There is another way, of course, which is not to take anything seriously.'

He knows what it's like to have nothing but faith to go on. He watches Olive walk with her head down and no shawl to protect her and thinks it unlikely he will see her again.

I try not to make too much noise in my life, he thinks. Does Olive have faith, I wonder?

'We never learn everything about the people we know,' he carries on calling out to her because he can't stop himself. 'It is part of our necessary separateness. We have so little influence. How we see people so often depends on what is inside us but, equally, we cannot know who we are without anyone to tell us.' The wind blows his words away.

I can't stop myself from going on even when I receive little encouragement, he thinks.

He later tells anyone who will listen, 'I could not stop myself from going on even though I received little encouragement. Her expression was as fathomless as the sea. I accomplished something but then again, nothing.'

He looks up at the sky again. The clouds have stopped scudding and are tinged with pink. It's one of the last light nights before the end of the summer and there are mosquitoes everywhere. He stands still for a long while then raises Olive's shawl above his head to attract her attention, hoping she will return for it or, at least, turn around, but Olive has disappeared from his sight as quickly as the rain has stopped. He hesitates for a moment before pushing the shawl into his pocket.

I was ridiculous, he thinks as he hangs the 'not open' sign above the library door. It might be time to get out of a place where you believe you know people but really know no-one. If I pass Olive in the street, I shall stop and speak to her.

He returns to his house in the town where he isn't particularly comfortable because he didn't grow up there.

Olive makes her way down the path she travelled only twenty minutes previously. The afternoon storm left branches cracking and falling all over the place and they scratch her face and obstruct her passage. However, these are the same trees she passed on her way to the library, they have been watching over her since they were saplings – they know her and won't cause her harm.

When she has walked a distance from the library she says, 'I am fine' – and hopes Alfred can hear her because she doesn't want to appear impolite.

Did I shake Alfred's hand? she wonders, I can't remember.

For a moment, she wishes her path led to Rose's house with its roses, sea green curtains and a marrow cake sitting under a mesh dome on the kitchen table but soon she approaches the sea, which has waited with all its power to accept her back and this makes sense to her like nothing else.

The sea is my friend, my life depends on it and it doesn't care who or what I am, she thinks.

When she opens her front door, the familiar sounds of wood shifting and scraping and the smell of moist salt rise up to greet her. They have never sounded or smelled better and she almost weeps with relief. There is movement and space here, she thinks, I can breathe – and my cat is pleased to see me.

She stands by her window for a while and watches the waves to see what they have to show her.

I am tired, she thinks, tired of hearing people's opinions. I am tired of hearing people say I am not normal when what they mean is, I am not like them. If I knew what I was looking for when I left home earlier, I did not find it in the library. I had planned to get everything straightened out and did nothing of the kind and I can't now think what pushed me to leave a place where the sea sings to me every time it washes the rocks.

She collapses on to her flowery sofa as if it were all she ever wanted. The smells of the storm linger on her and she still has her boots on. She thinks back on the day.

'Did I hope to make myself feel better by knowing Alfred had suffered?' she asks the waves.

She rocks back and forth, counting her movement till the sea silences her.

I am falling asleep, she thinks.

She dreams she is in the sea and waves are heaving her up and down. A huge wave rises, curls above her head and sends her crashing down into a watery world. The more she struggles, the further she is pushed. Then she hears a voice say 'stop. You can end this.

You don't have to do this' and it is the voice of a young Alfred Gorkin.

When she wakes, it is somewhere between night and day. She is still on her sofa and, thankfully, not in the sea.

Did I dream my visit to the library? she wonders, and will I wake from my dream to find I never left my sofa and sat staring at the sea?

She looks around to see whose house she is in then remembers that the house she is looking around – the wooden house perched on rocks above the sea – is the same one she has lived in for nearly fifteen years.

'I am home,' she tells the sea.

She returns to the library after that. She might decide to go for a walk and before she knows it, arrive at the library where she finds ways to remain undetected. She often waits for hours, feeling the pull of the place and thinking about what it would mean if she were to step inside again.

If the Ford Fiesta is there, she presses her nose to the window till she sees Alfred. If he is not at his desk, she stays, anyway, dreaming up things to say and never saying them.

Why do I go? she asks herself and decides she doesn't know except for not being able to shake off a sense of his wanting her to be there or of her wanting to be a part of his world and she only stops these visits when she realises that she goes to the library to unleash her anger and that anger is a worthless thing.

There is little point in standing next to a library all day, she thinks, loneliness is making me behave badly.

Alfred knows none of this. The one time he sees her and pushes open the door, she disappears. He thinks he sees her on another occasion, but apart from feeling strangely watched and wondering whether she has brought him something or returned for her shawl, he stays with his books. He is a quiet man and always has been and in all the years he has lived in the town, he has missed only four days' work.

The longer I remain in the town, the stranger I feel, he thinks. I think in a different language, anyway. I would hate to be a burden, but if someone were kind enough to visit, we might listen to

Beethoven's Emperor Concerto because Beethoven took pain and turned it into something beautiful.

Then one chilly day, he spends his time clearing out his house. This is all the time I need, he thinks. He wonders about leaving Olive an envelope of cash or writing her a letter explaining he can't be the father she wants but then he is not sure that this is what she wants so he changes his mind. He sells his car for a ridiculous price and picks up the two battered suitcases he keeps by his bed because one must be ready to leave at a moment's notice. He packs into them what he needs and disappears down the same road from which he entered the town, wearing his raincoat and trilby and planning never to return. He walks to the station and boards a train bound for the capital because life is about a refusal to be shamed.

'I chose to live in a place with small houses and small lives where little happens apart from working, living, ageing, dying and falling in and out of love,' he tells a fellow passenger. 'I chose to be among people who expressed no curiosity about my background and believed what they wanted to believe but I cannot remain in this town – one which is indistinguishable from so many others around it – even if I come to see in the future that this is what God wants for me. I am going to a new somewhere – I just did not think I would have to do so twice.'

No-one saw him leave – 'but then this town is not going to notice my exiting steps, even a town which said "welcome" all those years ago,' he continues.

After he departs, the sun's last rays set the sewing machines on his wall aglow but, apart from these, he leaves no more trace on the town than a smudge on a polished surface.

Have I solved anything or changed anything? he wonders as the train carries him away. Such questions have no answers. At least I have succeeded in not being swallowed up by history.

No truck or moving van arrives at his house. He seems to have evaporated out of it. When they unlock the front door, his books are gone and all they find is the worn armchair where he spent too much time, his computer, microwave oven, a photograph, an empty fridge and the sewing machines left – like bits of magic – in the sun.

News of his departure spreads. Some say, 'it's unbelievable. A man walked out of our town, carrying two suitcases and no-one saw him go. Is there a note?' Some even begin to wonder if he existed at all and some create a past for him. As he isn't there to argue the case for his life, a general frenzy prevails.

It is close to midnight when Alfred arrives in the capital city. Other Jewish exiles live there and his plan is to join them, but he will find he can no more go forward than back. It does worry him that the sense of loss he feels is because he might be someone people can't get to know.

What would have happened if I had proposed to Rose and she said yes? He wonders. My sense of loss has nothing to do with her. She was just another way I had of not feeling losses more painful to bear. I shall keep going on and when my time is up, God will come to fetch me and I shall recite 'Hear Oh Israel. The Lord our God, the Lord is one' while holding my right hand over my eyes to block out the world because I am no more able to stop being a Jew than to stop being myself.

On her final visit to the library, Olive sees his empty desk and chair. Where is Alfred? She wonders. Have I pushed him away?

When Rose tells her of his departure, Olive says, 'Oh help, oh help, this is terrible. This isn't how things were meant to turn out. It's all so difficult to accept. Does this have anything to do with me?' She shakes her head in disbelief. 'I have to do something – but what?' She decides she can't do anything to change things and doesn't have words to fit her feelings, anyway.

'Is Alfred now the grey cat which has begun to sit outside the library?' she asks Rose.

'When the time comes to leave, we leave and that's it,' replies Rose, who doesn't know about cats. She holds out her hands as if to push thoughts of cats away from her. Alfred must have been wanted elsewhere or he may have returned to the place of his childhood. I hope he doesn't find empty space there in place of his memories. This can happen, you know. Everything about him should have been clear but wasn't. God knows, he held my hand longer than usual when last we parted.'

God again, thinks Olive.

Rose sits alone for a long time with her head in her hands. Her heart hasn't been broken for, as far as she is concerned, Alfred was never anything more to her than a well-mannered gentleman. But she has lost something – a possibility, perhaps – something she knows won't come around again and, worse, she is left with the same feeling of responsibility she felt after Frank's death. Was there something I missed or could have done? she asks herself. In the end she decides there is nothing.

I wonder if he was dangerous in some way, she thinks before pushing the thought away and vowing, instead, to be kinder to people in the future – just like Alfred.

She enters his house – at last.

At least it's clean, she thinks, but is shocked to see how little he owned. She takes away the one photograph of him she finds; 'my way of remembering him,' she explains, 'it is clear to me he collected memories not things.'

Then she takes a bus to the library to return the book with hydrangeas on the cover she has not opened and has kept for too long. She decides to stick to books about roses in future and wonders if she will find one which shows her how to keep roses blooming through the autumn.

With words borrowed from the minister, she tells Olive, who is astonished that Alfred is simply gone, 'we are part of something bigger. You don't always end up in the place you planned. I hope I don't disappear or, worse, die before my time. Nina Simone died this year now I come to think about it.'

5
2004

Eight months have passed since Alfred disappeared and time is moving on. Even if she doesn't look old, Rose's greatest surprise is that she is no longer young.

I go on living the only way I know how – the way I have always done – which is to accept days and years being the same as the previous, she reflects – or it may just be that an angel urges me to keep living and I do.

She has cut her hair short and is leaving it to go the way of its natural grey rather than blonde and has been giving thought to selling her house and moving into sheltered housing – getting rid of everything and taking along just her rose bushes, wellington boots and a few recipe books.

I should give myself the boost of a change of surroundings because I could live another twenty years – but would I want to? she thinks.

The idea doesn't take shape or turn into anything like action because she worries about Olive returning to her lonely house after she has moved.

'The good thing about staying put,' she tells her neighbours, 'is I have somewhere to retreat to when the world outside is not to my liking or has let me down. I never feel alone because I see your lights clicking on and off and your heads bobbing up and down behind my roses – even if I never speak to anyone when I am in my garden.'

Although rows of roses continue to separate her garden from her neighbours on both sides, the town has changed and will keep changing long after she has gone. She barely recognises the streets outside her own. She is not indifferent to her town – in some ways its unassuming presence is responsible for the kind of life she leads, but she hasn't influenced developments in it and the people living there seldom come into her home.

No-one has the perfect life, she thinks and she consoles herself with this thought. She turns over in her mind the idea of the perfect life – whatever that is – but the idea evaporates as quickly as it rises.

Because her garden is showing the first signs of spring, she thinks about the months gone by and about the weather and about whether she feels weather changes more acutely than others or before others do. She also wonders whether she lives her life in a space closer to the weather than others do.

The past November was cold but cloudless and December, too and Rose's clothes were grey and lifeless.

'The sky's colour affects my mood,' she tells Olive, who doesn't need telling, 'and the months are turning over quicker than the time it takes to unbutton my coat.'

Olive marks passing days with crosses on her calendar and doesn't need to be told this either.

'When it rained for thirty days and nights I wondered if the rain was falling inside me and not somewhere outside. I can't take another drop. Summer seems like a dream. When I place my hands on the roses, I feel their sadness seeping through my gloves. How I manage to dig the flower beds with all this wet, I can't imagine,' Rose cries.

February brings rain and more rain and it feels as if both the town and its people are washed clean. When March comes around, the air is saturated. April proves to be an unpredictable grey month with grey skies when the wind blows blossoms from trees and hats off heads.

Now April has become May, Rose can smell the weather changing as skies brighten, the sea turns from black to green and forecasts are for milder weather to come.

On a particularly beguiling Tuesday, when the sky is pale and unruffled and the sun dries out her garden before strolling into her house, Rose opens her eyes on her seventy-fifth birthday to the strange and lovely sensation that her life is cloudless. In the months just passed, there have been times when she has felt herself pass from one thing to the next with her capacity for joy diminished. But now, she's happy with small gifts like the scent of hyacinths, the patterns of spring light on her floor and the fact that the town's crocuses match the mauve and yellow skies.

Because she has much to be thankful for, she invites all the people who live in her street to a tea party to celebrate her birthday. She includes Eric, the young man who arrived from nowhere to help in her garden when a fall in the supermarket put her temporarily out of action, the minister who buried Frank and Pamela, the librarian who replaced Alfred. Most guests knew Frank – although there are one or two who didn't and she plans to offer them tea, cakes, sandwiches and home-made marrow wine.

She contemplates her house; once the bright colour of one of Frank's eyes, it looks washed out now. Wisteria sprawls up its walls and over the roof and almost covers the two large bay windows. On the inside it is painted white and most of the objects in it – including the carpets and some of the chairs – have remained in place for more than half a century. She hasn't redecorated since Frank died and doesn't plan to.

'I simply move dust around from wherever it has settled,' she tells Olive.

Rose starts her day by washing her windows – a task begun the night before and as she cleans the glass, the sun, which seems to express the same radiance she is feeling, wipes away the tail end of the winter chill and gives its blessing of warmth to the walls, carpets and sea-green curtains. She puts on her glasses and dusts and polishes, taking her time with her cloth over Frank's wooden angels – because it is in them that he lives on, she thinks. Then she moves to the watercolours her father painted and places vases of spring flowers on every possible surface.

If ever there were a day for it, this is a day for thinking, she tells herself. She pushes aside a stray roller which is pulling a damp curl over her glasses then rubs her cloth over the mirror in the hall; 'this isn't me,' she says to the old woman staring back at her.

The cleaning done, she decides to hop on the two buses necessary to take her to the graveyard so she can remind Frank of her birthday and let him know that although she misses him, she is nonetheless grateful to be alive.

'Hello Frank,' she begins as she walks towards his grave. She runs a tentative hand over the headstone engraved with the words 'loving husband and father' then picks a sprouting shoot from the rose bush she's planted nearby and places it on top of the stone.

'It's my birthday, Frank,' she says.

She kneels then takes a handkerchief out of her pocket and polishes the stone.

'It's not that I miss you because you never leave me,' she continues softly lest she disturb his spirit or any nearby angels busy doing things. She wishes she could be sure of some sort of life after life.

'It's just that I may not have thanked you when I could see you and I hope you won't now tell me it's too late. The weather is as good as it can be after all the rain and the rose beds are soggy but that's all right.'

A purple pigeon which has been strutting around in the sand beside her holds her in its gaze before flying to the top of a nearby pine tree. The image of Frank slumped over his steering wheel has been with her all morning but because she has a strong sense of being guided, she takes the bird's fluttering to be her husband's soaring spirit. She stands up and brushes the dirt off her skirt – job done. Time to go home and check that the cakes she left in the oven have not exploded while her back was turned.

The cakes have never risen so well. She watches them till they double in size and the whole house smells of cake - which is a lovely smell.

Things of beauty, she thinks.

Once again she shapes marzipan back and forth till she has made roses which she places on top of the cakes. She then folds her napkins, sets glasses out on a tray and positions her chairs; eight people will sit comfortably and one, uncomfortably, she thinks.

Her thoughts turn to her appearance because she has always cared about how she looks. She decides to wear the cream dress patterned with blue roses which Frank liked; she has had it for decades and can still squeeze into it.

I still see things in terms of his likes and dislikes, she reflects.

She pins an enamel brooch of a basket of roses onto the dress just below her right shoulder, shades her eyelids blue to match the roses, paints her lips with Dusky Pink and changes her mind about wearing a rose covered hat. Finally, she locks her bedroom door because she doesn't want coats on the bed she once shared with Frank.

At 3.30 on this day in May, when there is a rainbow in the sky and Rose is glancing at her wristwatch and wondering what to do next, the doorbell announces Olive and the other guests, all of whom seem to arrive at the same time.

When Olive walks into the room, she feels no curiosity about anyone else, but still shakes hands all round before sitting in a corner between Eric and the minister who winks at her as if they shared a secret. She would have preferred to remain standing but doesn't want to draw attention to herself and she hopes no-one will come up and ask how she is feeling because too much asking makes her feel queasy.

People step on Rose's floral carpet, asking, 'all right Rose?' or calling out 'many happy returns' or 'your house is most unusual' or 'how sad Frank is not here' because very little can be said to Rose without mentioning Frank's death when all she wants is for people to treat her like they did when he was alive.

'All fine,' answers Rose and 'thank you' and 'thank you, again' and 'yes it is sad.'

Then they stand around eating egg sandwiches and meringues filled with cream and balancing cups or glasses and Pamela, the new librarian keeps dabbing her lips so not to leave lipstick marks on her cup.

Rose is imagining Frank walking from room to room when the minister says, 'it's spring but the sun is struggling to stay around.'

As this party might be her last – because you never know – Rose offers thanks for the weather; she was so sure the afternoon would be drowned out by rain.

Her guests appear to know who they are and be sure of what they want – how little she understands others – and she thinks about the sadness which comes from not knowing what secrets other people hold in their hearts.

When she turns off the lights and carries in the pink and white cake, shaped as a rose, of course and decorated with her marzipan roses, she says, 'Time for birthday cake,' and they all sing 'Happy Birthday to you' and toast her and her roses while making private wishes for health and love and money.

This is one of those special days which make sense of all the rest, she thinks. She taps a spoon against a glass. 'Cheers to life – whatever that means,' she says, 'you can't get the better of life because you'd be surprised how fast the years go by.' She keeps this statement running through her head because it won't harm her – not today.

For a time everyone sips their drinks in silence pretending they do this every day while the sun drifts off once more and the sky changes from yellow to grey. They all try to hide their eagerness to stare at Olive about whom they've heard so much.

Olive smiles her beautiful smile.

The few clothes Olive possesses are mostly green but today she is wearing her beige dress printed all over with pink flamingos which look as if they might detach themselves from the fabric and fly off at any moment. Her legs stick to each other through her tights and her hair is braided and piled on top of her head. Her feet are bound up in sandals. She arrived at the party with her cat and she positions it on top of her feet so no-one will see them.

'Who is that young stranger?' asks the minister breaking the silence and pointing to Eric. 'It's no coincidence that he's here. The tide must have brought him in' and he laughs a solitary laugh.

Rose doesn't reply because she's wondering if beige is Olive's colour. She, herself, never wears beige. It's difficult to know where she ends and Olive begins.

Did I say that out loud? she wonders, because Olive appears to have heard.

Olive is busy apologising in her head for the lack of symmetry between her feet for she senses that people are pretending not to notice and this is what she is busy doing when Eric raises his glass to her.

'I am Eric,' he says although he knows that she knows. 'You have a mysterious smile and it makes your face shine.' The more he watches, the more beautiful she becomes.

Eric is slim and graceful, his hair is long and tied back in a ponytail and his cheeks are sunburned under his freckles. When he sees that Olive's left foot is stiff and turned inward and clamped under her cat, he looks away. 'Your sandals are too tight. You will destroy your feet,' he says.

His words feel like sea-foam on sand and Olive lets them wash around the room before landing where she can grab them and put them in her pocket.

'It was my lucky day when Eric walked up to my roses. Have another slice of cake, Eric,' says Rose, gulping down a second glass of marrow wine. 'Olive, cut him another slice of cake but mind the marzipan roses.'

The sun sweeps back through the room like a searchlight.

While she has prepared herself for this day, all Olive can think is that she misses the sea.

Rose watches her cut into the cake and thinks it is only and was always the two of us, taking it in turns to be angry, calming each other down and limiting each other. As far as I am concerned, Olive is the only person in the room. If she has known unhappiness and loneliness, don't most people?

There are nine people in this room, thinks Olive, fewer than I expected - and they all seem to have grinning faces. There were thirty-two mourners at Frank's funeral. Have twenty-three people died, moved away or lost interest?

'Happy birthday, Rose,' she remembers, continuing to look around the room as she hands her mother a necklace she has made from pink and white shells. 'You always liked pink.'

Olive never looks people straight in the eye. But now, she makes an effort as she doesn't want to be considered rude. She lets herself be looked at, she lets herself be kissed – but it makes her feel threatened.

'Thanks, I love them. Thank you again,' says Rose in as carefree a manner as possible because she wants to show how far she has moved from the slightly preposterous fantasy that every time she returns home, Olive will be there waiting. The trick, she has found, is not to want this so much.

Rose drapes the shells around her neck next to her pearls which is how Olive knows she likes the necklace. Then she sits back and thinks, life is something to celebrate and listens to the words which have begun drifting across her room.

People talk about children and grandchildren and about who has died in the past year. They bite into happiness which is the taste of Rose's cake. The lady who lives in the yellow house on Rose's left seldom leaves her house but when she does, she spends her time watching Rose.

'What huge hyacinths you have,' she says, 'what do you feed them?' Then she licks icing off her fingers and continues without addressing anyone in particular and as if she were talking to the cake, 'is that the minister from Frank's funeral? Let's ask him what to do about the war.'

'Which war?' Olive asks.

'Did you need to respond to that, Olive?' the minister suggests, trying to be kind.

'Not really,' she replies.

The woman who lives on Rose's right, painted her house violet because her name is Violet. She's hovering in a cloud of pity and tells Rose she would have written had she known Frank died – even though she knew – then she bursts into tears.

'Is everything well with you now, Rose?' she asks, dabbing her eyes with a lace handkerchief.

'Oh well, you know, not bad, not bad,' answers Rose who's checking her carpet for tea stains.

Violet leans forward and points at Olive. She likes to believe she knows everything about everyone in the town.

'What I think,' she says from her place on Edith's rocking chair, 'is that all of us are fumbling around – trying to do the best we can, but I would say that that girl is not right.'

That is your opinion and it's not important, thinks Rose, who has her own way of looking at things. How does Violet manage to find her path into everything – to live in the gaps in other peoples' lives?

Rose drains her glass. Marrow wine has made her brave. 'What do you do all day, Violet?' she sniffs although she has little interest in the answer.

Pamela looks on. She has chosen to sit on the arm of the sofa next to the minister and her handbag swings from the crook of her arm.

'My name is Pamela,' she tells him. When she extends her hand, her bent arm makes her look slightly lop-sided. A yellow butterfly rising from a buddleia in the garden distracts her. 'Sorry,' she continues, 'sorry – but it is lovely to see yellow after the particularly grey winter just passed – and spring can be as grey as winter.'

'What's wrong with grey?' asks Olive.

Silence descends again except for the sounds of forks scraping against plates.

'Everybody is always going through something,' says the minister, breaking through the quiet once more, 'but life changes in ways we can't imagine.' He pats Olive's arm.

'I am not used to parties. Did you say chocolate cake?' he asks Rose.

Rose did not so she shakes her head, smiles as if she understands his request and fills up his teacup instead.

He listens with his ears but not his heart – and even his ears deceive him, she thinks.

'People who are missed by others go to heaven; fact.'

There he is – still talking.

'I'm sorry. Could you repeat that?' asks Pamela.

Rose turns to see if Olive's listening but Olive is pretending not to hear. Her plait is drooping a little – coming undone at the side and Rose begins to worry that her daughter looks shrunken, somehow, in her bird-filled dress. She wants to cry at the speed with which childhood passes.

'Shall we all move on to something stronger than tea?' she asks because she herself has done so. 'Let's drink to the future – the future is all ahead of us. Come on Olive!'

'Yes, give her something to drink,' says Violet.

'I don't drink,' says Olive.

'I shouldn't tell anyone,' laughs Rose.

'Tell anyone what?' asks Olive who has been counting the number of times Pamela says 'sorry'.

Rose is becoming tipsy. 'What do you think of the marrow wine?' she asks.

'I haven't tried it,' says Olive.

The sun drops into the distant sea and Olive can stand the noise no longer. She makes her excuses, ties her shawl around her and walks out of the room with her cat so she can go from where people are to where they are not.

'Let's put on some dance music,' says Rose, who doesn't see her go, 'you can't have a party without dancing.'

She stands in the middle of the room and sways to the music, waving her hands in the air so that they looked like wings. The minister taps his feet on the carpet but no-one joins in her dance so her hands flutter back to her sides and she returns to her chair. The strain of the party is beginning to show. When did I become someone no-one could see? she thinks before hearing the front door close.

'Won't you stay a little longer Olive? Olive?' she calls to the door.

My life is filled with Olive one minute and strangers the next, she thinks.

'Where is Olive going now?' asks Violet.

Everyone rises.

They have all been moved by the sight of Rose in her floral dress and all have ideas about how she should live her life or what she should do with her house and they walk out saying, 'keep cheerful', and 'a lick of paint will do the job' and 'we'll see you very soon.' Pamela says 'thank you – and sorry' and walks away with her handbag swinging from her arm.

Before he leaves the house, the minister says, 'I, myself, have just this morning entered my sixty-third year on earth. Thank you for the lovely chocolate cake – terrible for the body but good for the soul.' He has developed the habit of saying things people want to hear and speaks so emphatically that Rose begins to wonder who of them is wrong. When he taps her on the hand she feels forgiven although she doesn't know for what.

She says, 'I can't thank you enough for coming. It's been I don't know how long since someone was in the house. Don't forget your coat.'

The day has disappeared like sand through my fingers, she thinks when she contemplates her empty house. All in all, my party has gone well and I am glad of this as I worried I might be thought of as someone who was living as if it were still 2000 and Frank were still alive.

She tries not to look at the hyacinths she can smell fading in their vases because, if she does, she will have to do something about them. When she climbs the stairs to her bedroom, she's alone. She slips first out of her noisy dress then out of her party shoes, hoping to save the leather for another day; they can't stand too much wear, she thinks. Then she reflects on her guests one by one and wonders if the hum she hears is Olive calling out to her from across the waves. But winter, it seems, hasn't given up entirely, it has turned cold and wet again and the hum is just the wind. She shuts her window because rain is falling on to her carpet. What shall I do with the rest of my birthday cake? she wonders.

Olive walks home with her cat. When she reaches her house, it is no longer a fine spring evening. The rain stopped just long enough to allow the sun to warm Rose's party and now it has started again, falling all around her while the wind whips the waves so high, they smash against the rocks and send sea spray over the windows.

There on her threshold is Eric hoping, perhaps, for something even he doesn't understand.

'Hello Olive,' he says.

Because it is raining so hard, she can make out only shapes not sounds and wonders, at first, who he is.

'Hello Olive,' he says again.

When she hears him speak a second time, she asks, 'how did you find me?' and she stands before him confused and not knowing what to do.

She listens for his voice under the rain which splashes on to her crooked foot and wets her braids till tangled strands of hair hang limply down her forehead.

'I love the rain,' she continues when he doesn't reply, 'how long have you been out here?'

'Say again' asks Eric because he can't hear above the water's noise.

'How long have you been here?' she repeats.

'I don't know. I don't have a watch,' he replies but doesn't laugh, 'may I come in?'

'Yes,' she says, 'as long as you don't stay long.'

'Are you sure?' is his reply. Olive strikes him as strange – strange and attractive, 'I like your house, by the way. It could be a boat sailing to anywhere.'

Eric speaks as if standing on tiptoe. 'Are you with anyone?' he asks.

His words feel like chocolate melting in her mouth. She answers, 'no' and nearly bursts into tears.

'I don't know why it's you and not someone else,' he says, 'but I like you. I feel I know all about you. It's as simple as that. I know that if you say you like me too, that'll be how it is for both of us – for now, at any rate.'

Olive lets the rain run from her hair on to her dress.

Then, hesitant as spring sunlight, Eric places his hands on either side of her face and kisses her. 'You are lovely as a rose,' he says.

Olive feels a whoosh of healing go down to her crooked foot and doesn't know what to do about it. She imagines she is a rosebush sending up its buds to bloom all over her body.

Her cat licks her legs and curls himself around her and she pushes him aside.

'Get away, cat,' she says, shivering in the rain.

The cat hisses and froths.

Eric follows her into her wooden home and closes the door on the cat which bounds towards the sea, making sprinting look easy and hoping, perhaps, to return when they have finished.

Olive's dress is crumpled and wet. She takes it off and it drops to the floor. She un-plaits her hair and it tumbles over her shoulders. When Eric kisses the top of her head, the scents of wood and sea float up to him making him want to put aside everything he has ever lost and everything he has ever gained before this time.

Across the bay, Rose stands beside her bed and says her prayers before lying down under her pink quilt and falling asleep, happy. She dreams of spring, of trees sagging under white blossoms and of seagulls gliding soundlessly across purple skies.

When she wakes the next morning, the rain has stopped and sunlight is back in her house.

At the same time, Eric walks away from Olive's house thinking of her delightful strangeness. Salt air fills his nose, the sun is round and hopeful, and a plane is flying overhead. He imagines the people seated in it. Because places spit him out and force him to move around, nothing lifts his spirit like the sight of an aeroplane carrying people away from somewhere to somewhere across a summer sky.

He loved Olive as much as he could love anyone while knowing full well that love doesn't have to enter these things. She has an innocence you don't often see, he thinks, but the awareness she showed along with it was almost shocking.

In the pink of her happiness – and with Eric now gone, Olive drapes her shawl around her and goes outside to smell the sea – as specific as a human being – and call out for her cat.

She soaked up Eric's love like the sand soaks up sea. She suspects him of having other women but did not want to ask. What matters is that she finally gave in and spent a night with a man. This was also the first time I undressed anyone besides myself, she thinks.

But something isn't right.

In her life, the whole and the broken seem to come along in the same package. She suddenly feels that this special day might be shaped by disaster before a policeman with dark bags of sadness under his eyes walks into her garden and asks, 'who lives here?'

He sees a woman with a crooked foot wearing a shawl.

'Only me,' she replies.

'How are you this morning?' he continues.

'I am fine. Why do you ask?'

And then he says that he saw a cat's head rise again and again above the choppy water before being washed up on the beach. He is the sort of man who is usually calm, but lack of sleep makes him jumpy and his eyes keep travelling from Olive's face to her foot – although he does his best to control them.

As he offers her the corpse in a cardboard box, he says, 'I don't want to bother you with details, but the force of the water must have pushed the cat down. If the sea continues like this, it will claim another life. Is this cat yours?'

Olive shakes her head in disbelief and takes the animal in her arms. She says 'thank you' although she is not sure why.

'This is terribly sad,' he says.

Then Olive weeps tears for the life that might have been. She rocks back and forth. She can't do anything else. The noise of her weeping circles the bay and passes over Rose's roses before returning limply to her feet.

After a heart-breaking time during which she becomes tired out from weeping, Olive climbs on to a high rock with the cat in her arms and looks down on to the beach. Is that Frank's ghost sitting on the sand, asking about the cat? she wonders. What is it doing there? It takes a while for her to realise that it is no ghost but Pamela, the harmless librarian, waving from under a hat.

'Sorry, it's me, Pamela,' she calls out.

Look at the state of me, thinks Olive as she carries the cat away with her to find a place to bury it.

Rose has had one of her long baths and smells like a rose but hasn't brushed her hair. She moved around a lot the day before – baking, feeding, wiping, – and tiredness has draped itself around her like a damp towel. I feel like a dormant sea, she thinks.

She decides not to worry about writing thank you notes on her pink notepaper with roses on the borders. Instead, she drinks four cups of tea, puts on her blue towelling dressing gown and sits down in front of her television with a tray of toast and marrow jam on her lap. The sun lights up the hyacinths dying in their vase as she watches two lifeguards carry a lifeless cat – whose cat? she wonders – out of the sight of early morning bathers. The newsman says the seas around are so turbulent they will become increasingly full of death. Rose opens a window and leans out as far as she can to check.

When Olive rings, she knows that Rose has never thought of herself as an animal person and that she doesn't care about cats – not really – but she rings her all the same.

No surprise that Rose is staring once more at her hyacinths when she hears the phone ring. She felt a disturbance of energy in the room before the ring. She is often fearful these days. She strikes a match and lights a cigarette before answering because smoking brings her calm.

'Hello Olive,' she says, pressing the receiver between her shoulder and good ear. 'What is it? What day is it?' The day might be Wednesday but Rose isn't sure. 'Are you all right?'

'No.'

'Why are you calling me?'

Olive takes a moment to arrange sentences in her head.

'I am calling about my cat – my drowned cat. He had been my friend all my life. I brought him with me to your party. I called for him this morning. "Cat, cat," I called, but there was no answer.'

'Oh Olive, oh love,' says Rose.

Olive has always loved animals and I should let her be, she thinks. After all, I am the only woman in the town to speak of angels as if they shared living space with everybody else.

'Let's not panic Olive. Don't worry. I'm sure it won't be long before another cat arrives at your door.'

For a moment, daughter and cat merge in her mind. It's her nerves. 'Why don't you get another cat?'

Rose's words spring to life and scratch her daughter's skin. It's like that between them – not anger, exactly – but irritation.

Olive stays silent.

Olive spends the week after that alternating between mourning and reliving her night with Eric. It is only when an experience is behind her that she can work out what she feels about it and she becomes aware of how tired she is – wanting to spend a night with a man for so long made her tired even if she told herself she didn't care – not to mention the loss of her pet.

When Eric returns a week later with a rose in his hand, Olive asks, 'is this for me?' She might have asked 'where have you been?' She might have said, I missed you.' She might've told him to leave because she has waited for him – even if waiting is what she does so often, it begins to feel less like waiting and more like what life is. She might ask if he loves her but she doesn't do any of these things because she's afraid to know the truth.

'I think about you all the time,' he says, and his words wrap themselves around her like a shawl. 'You are not like other girls and I like people who are different. With no special place to call home, I suppose I must be different, too.'

He is a person cut off – like she is. He lets nothing stick. An odd jobber, who is good at fixing things, he has always moved from town to town like tumbleweed, looking for jobs which require neither qualifications nor experience. He gathers adventures, not friends.

'Something once forced me to be on the move although I can't put a name to it,' he explains. 'My father was a boat builder and what mattered once to me was going into his trade but now, while I know about the gap between who I am and who I should be, I am a person cut off just the same.'

Olive thinks they should talk about this because they have the time and are together but she can't bring herself to do so. Instead, she says, 'everybody around me seems to die. Promise me you won't.'

He looks at her as if she has no idea how much she is asking.

The two of them take off their shoes and climb down the rocks which shine pink and grey in the sunshine. Love – or is it gratitude – agrees with Olive. Why wouldn't it? She gladly uncovers her feet and wades into the sea, stepping from one rock pool to another and not minding if she slips on seaweed.

Then Eric hoists her on to his back and carries her home because he can – and Olive holds on to his strength, his eyes and his spirit.

When they return to her house, Olive looks at the cushion where cat is not and says, 'poor cat. While we were tossing about inside, he was outside being tossed by the waves,' and her tears bubble up and taste like the sea.

'Am I making a fool of myself?' she asks.

'No,' he replies and offers her a cigarette which she nearly takes.

His phone begins to vibrate with text messages which he ignores at first but when he checks them, he says, 'I've entered your life just as past lives are preventing me. Do you like people? I don't,' and he looks up from his phone.

Olive doesn't answer, but watches as he walks out of her door to a new somewhere because he must – he can't help himself – this is what he does.

She doesn't follow but calls out, 'things have made me different. Things matter to me more than they do to other people. You don't like my limp – but then, nor do I. This isn't the worst thing. The only difference is you walk away from it while I'll carry my limp around with me for the rest of my life.'

A piece of paper pushed under her door the next day is her only reminder that Eric existed. She grabs it from the floor and sits on her sofa to read his clumsy scrawl.

'I have to go away for a time as I can't be in two places at once,' he writes. 'I shall think of you and your smile and your house near the rocks. I expect I'll be back but all I can be sure of is I've had too many experiences of having to pick up and move on and here is another.'

The note isn't signed and there is nothing Olive can do – absolutely nothing.

His words assume life, jump off the paper, slap her in the face and bounce around her house before dropping into the sea and taking away with them something of who she is and something she is not.

He may as well not have existed, she thinks, and it doesn't help matters that there's nothing in his note which a part of me didn't suspect.

It's of no concern to her to know that Eric wanted to tell her his story of moving on but decided against it because the story was connected to a greater, sadder story he didn't know how to explain. And she doesn't need to know that he'll drift from job to job or that he'll assume – wrongly – that she'll forget him. It's just his nature.

Olive rings Rose to tell her that life is so much easier when it's just her foot keeping her hurt.

'Who is Eric, anyway?' says Rose, who knew something was wrong because all her roses withered overnight. 'Who is anyone? People leave us, I'm sad to say. Sometimes you look away and things change. Some men fall in love with one woman followed by the next. I should forget Eric. Life – it never ends. It's one thing after another but you have to live through certain things before you understand them.'

These days, nobody seems to stay with us for very long, she thinks.

At this time, Olive has no understanding of how sad and difficult it is to end a friendship with someone who hasn't died because she hasn't been in such a situation before. She feels as sorry for herself as a bird with a broken wing.

'What I do know is that grief is back again. I recognise it from the first time around,' she tells Rose, 'how do other people handle these things?'

A thought strikes and Rose asks, 'might Eric have lied to you?'

'Why would he?' answers Olive.

'Everybody does,' Rose answers.

The last few months have been a bit much, she thinks.

'One loss doesn't protect you from others,' she says, never sure why her thoughts go the way they do.

Beyond keeping more of an eye on her garden than usual because you never know, she thinks, Eric might return when we're busy doing other things, she determines not to have anything further to do with him.

Olive decides Eric will be the only man for her even if she discovered little about him. She doesn't know if he likes to walk or if he likes the colour green, if he prefers the sea or sunshine or if his father is alive. For a while, he is the focus of her every thought and because he has taken up residence in her head and because she is sure he will return, she follows every man she sees in case it's him. But soon her thinking about him becomes more important to her than his departure, and she learns to live quite well without him. All she tells Rose about the night they spent together is that the rain made the flamingos trickle down her dress and that her cat drowned.

There will come a time when Eric will return to the town on a warm, still April day. He will see Olive on the beach and they will look at each other like strangers, at first, before spending one last night together. He will be surprised to find everything just as he remembered – especially Olive and she will hear him say he has never stopped thinking about her.

She will reply that she hasn't had sex with anyone else because nobody can take his place in her bed which is nothing special – just a simple sofa with scatter cushions on it facing the sea.

He will want to talk about the time they've spent apart but she won't. She will then walk away wishing she had mentioned the fact that he had been important to her and that while nothing much happened, it was something.

'Eric might be over,' she tells Rose, 'but that doesn't mean Eric never happened. You could say I found happiness and lost it again. That is all.'

She begins to associate happiness with rain – after Eric – although she can't be expected to know that Eric is not his real name.

'Happiness,' tries Rose who is not one for thoughts about happiness, 'is an impossible state to maintain but isn't it extraordinary how ordinary life has a way of going on even when you think you can't? You have the sea, Olive, and it's a still point among so much change.'

As far as the sea is concerned, it continues journeying up and down the beach because it doesn't distinguish between happiness and sadness and has no interest at all in lives struggling to maintain impossible states.

6

2005

The year becomes 2005. The earth and sky remain unchanged. Rose has turned seventy-six and Olive, thirty-six. Life, which continues as a random succession of loss with the occasional appearance of joy, is moving them mainly forwards, as it must, but, at times, seems to be moving them towards the past and Rose still wakes on the occasional night fearing she might find someone she loves – Olive, say, dead in a car in the time it takes for her to put on the kettle.

Had Frank lived, this would have been our fifty-second year together, thinks Rose, but I mustn't think this way.

'Things change,' she tells Olive, 'I don't know how they change or why, but change they do – and without your wanting this or even realizing it. I could choose sadness, or I could choose joy but that won't stop things changing.'

She has all but forgotten about her party, which, God knows, wasn't an event of great consequence, she thinks, but it was followed by a time of kindness between neighbours and between her and Olive.

Although I live in a town where many people are solitary, solitude is making me strange, she thinks. I wake too early and spend too much time cleaning now because there is always so much to clean and the dust in the house is so difficult to control. It's a story without end.

The best I can do is to keep on living as Frank did – accepting kindness and the quiet ordinariness of things and being more inclined to see that Olive's peculiarity – if such it is – leads straight to me.

She tells herself all this while pulling up weeds and dead-heading roses but her accepting kindness doesn't stop her from missing Frank and – the last thing she expected – Alfred Gorkin too, although not in the same way, of course.

She and Olive have fallen into the habit of walking together most days and Rose tells her things she thinks she should know about life or loss or joy. 'It's only how I see it,' explains Rose and she never asks Olive questions.

Olive asks, 'how are you Rose?' but doesn't say much more.

Olive is older, of course, and has all but stopped her nocturnal walking, but her smile still has the sun in it. Another stray cat has found its way to her home and she cares for it as lovingly as anyone can and remains as devoted as ever to her town.

Saturdays in the town are important. Saturdays are market days. In a place where the noise is mostly sea melody, this day is marked by different sounds. Things come to life around eight when the day is made official by the sounds of metal shop shutters rising and vans stuffed full of goods creaking their way up too narrow streets and farmers, fishermen, housewives, craftsmen all shouting 'hello again!', hey there!' and 'how was your week?' while the sea continues to splash away in the distance.

On a particularly cold, murky Saturday in mid-October when electric lights stay on all day and the wind rips up leaves, the sun rises on Rose's and Olive's lives. Rose puts on a yellow coat over a cotton dress and adds an orange scarf, thick socks and the same wellington boots she has worn for the thirty years the sun has risen on her garden. She wears glasses all the time now – the better to see her roses, although she can't work in the garden today because the cold is such, she can smell it.

She walks out of her front door with as much bounce as she can muster and wearing the self she wears for town, before realising she has left her handbag on the hall floor. She re-enters her house and re-crosses the hall before walking out again – this time, with her handbag tucked under her arm.

'Here I go again,' she tells herself as she makes her way down the drive which is not so much a drive as a space for walking between rose bushes where they once parked their car.

Her plan is to sell her marrow jam and the last of her roses in the market but the chilly breeze which blew through her window during the night left her with stiff shoulders and she needs Olive's help.

The two women meet in the High Street where wind is whipping up plastic bags into windscreens, tea is brewing all over and sails flap wildly in the distance. The thought of selling or shopping unnerves Olive who feels Rose's presence before she sees her.

'This wind could knock a person down,' says Rose as she struggles up the sloping street towards her daughter.

Olive bends towards her mother and her arms go around her shoulders and the cardigan which was Frank's. She smiles into her mother's hair and the two of them walk to their stall. There is motion all around. Cars jam car parks and side streets, stands are erected and everything under the sun is displayed from home-made cheeses to dishtowels, volleyballs and bats, booties, lamb chops and batteries while stray bits of garbage twirl in the light; even the policeman who visited Olive runs a stall selling cuttings from his garden because this helps him forget facts like the one that he returned a dead cat to her weeping owner a year ago.

The smells of the town come rolling at Rose and Olive – the coffee, salt, baking smells and people and everyone is going through strange, private motions – putting on a show of living in the town.

Olive limps her way along and Rose maintains her distance. They stop first to look at bits of old china and the policeman's cuttings before positioning themselves behind their own display table. With her tongue wedged in the side of her mouth, Rose concentrates on putting her jam in pots and on little plastic spoons for tasting.

She has baked a marrow cake which she places in the centre of the table before throwing in the last of her roses which she asks Olive to arrange in jam jars around the cake.

Olive can't make the simplest decisions today – where to put the jars and how many stems to place in each. She drops a glove, knocks a jar and sends water spilling everywhere.

'What's the matter with you?' asks Rose who has been thinking about the parts of the town she hardly visits. She doesn't know who lives there or their reasons for so doing and she dreads the possibility of having to depend on the indifference of strangers.

She doesn't wait for Olive's answer. Listening isn't her strong point.

People they don't know mill around and the first shoppers begin arguing over roses and jams and about which is the sweetest. Olive shoos away the gulls which have tumbled down from the roof of the shop behind them on to their stall.

'Don't go spoiling things here. Go back to the sea,' she tells them.

Rose's orange scarf and yellow coat make her look like she is wearing the sun and Olive is draped, as usual, in a green shawl with gloves to match, but at least the anger she once felt doesn't seem to be connected to her any longer.

They sit on their stools cradling mugs of coffee and eating almond and cherry slices. Rose asks customers how they are doing, hands over a pot of jam or a bunch of roses, says 'there you go,' rearranges jars and spoons to fill the spaces and when she and Olive are alone, lights a celebratory cigarette.

She has started saying, 'I'm an old lady now – I have had enough, to be honest,' but on other days, she says, 'I may be seventy-six, but can still have fun.'

This is one such day, she thinks, and I feel full of gratitude to strangers – however little I may know about them. Today is turning into one of those days when we could be any two women spending time together in the only place we could possibly be, and happiness is moving through me like sunlight.

A worn-out image of Frank with his mismatched eyes walking towards her with his carpenter's apron on under his overcoat, suddenly comes to her. She quickly pushes away the brief feeling of sadness which comes with it. It's been four years since Frank died but she has not yet managed to think of him without unravelling a little and she wants to hold on to the day's happiness.

She swirls coffee around her mouth before asking, 'my memory is becoming unreliable. It has a mind of its own. Have you noticed?'

'No. But, yes, I think I have,' replies Olive who doesn't know what to do with the expression she sees on her mother's face and who wants to be nice to her.

That's life, thinks Rose.

'That's life,' says Olive.

Rose's cigarette sends smoke up from a saucer. She stares at it in the odd, abstracted way she has developed over the past year then dabs at a rogue splash of coffee on the display table. She draws on the cigarette and passes it on to Olive who does the same and Rose, who suppresses a crazy desire to sing 'Feeling Good' just as Nina Simone sang, wishes they could just sit there for ever.

'I am glad you're here,' she says because Olive looks, for a moment, like the young woman who once carried her possessions to her new home across the sand.

Olive feels a deep and bewildering sense of responsibility for her mother whose rose-like fragility has always distinguished her from other mothers, but who looks particularly old and small suddenly as if she might disappear. The thought hasn't entered her head that Rose might die and the thing she wants most in the world is for this not to happen. She looks at her tired face as if she doesn't know who she is. She does know. She also realises that she will lose her one day. They leave the conversation about Rose's memory waiting to be picked up another time.

When did she start wearing glasses? Olive thinks.

'Please don't die,' she says.

A lost memory of her sitting in the Morris Minor eating Neapolitan ice cream with Frank surfaces for Rose. Here he is again. Everything about him continues to live on in her.

She closes her eyes and says, 'Olive, you are the smell of a rainbow, the breeze through trees and the promise of sunshine. Without you, I'd be as lonely as a lighthouse. What else is there to say?'

How nice that sounds, she thinks.

'Thank you,' says Olive with her beautiful smile, 'dear God.'

'All right, Olive?' asks Rose trying to read Olive's thoughts from her hand held tight around her cup. It's hard to know what pleases her. Olive takes up so much space in her head, it's exhausting.

'I'm okay. I'm not bad, not bad at all,' replies Olive.

Rose tries to picture what Olive sees – numbers of jars and plates and tea towels added to so many trays of meat and shoppers and seagulls and flowers. As far as she's concerned, Olive is a 'closed book'.

The past positions itself next to her and she thinks again of Frank. He was never as real for her in life as he has become in death.

He was always a solitary person, anyway, she tells herself, albeit one who was strong and smiling. Is that him beckoning to her from the other side of the road?

She is sure she sees a vision of him walking up the hill, carrying something wrapped up in his coat but she can't be sure what.

When she shares this with Olive, Olive becomes angry because Rose hasn't said Frank's name out loud for a time and is doing so now in a way which she considers disrespectful. Olive doesn't say anything.

'Do you remember Frank's hands? Do you remember Frank's hands bent around a wooden angel?' Rose tries again and leans forward for emphasis. 'Did I tell you about the wooden angels Frank carved?'

'No,' answers Olive, who, of course, knows about the wooden angels.

'Would you like me to tell you?' Rose continues.

Olive nods then asks, 'could you not?' as she prefers to think, instead, about the pink light of evening marking the veins on Frank's hands, or about the same hands holding hers in a walk along the beach or resting on his grey carpenter's apron.

They agree that Frank was a loner, but the things Rose remembers are different from the things Olive remembers so they sit for a while with their different, silent memories.

'Do you remember the day Frank put his coat around my shoulders because I never carry an umbrella or wear a hat – as you know – and this left him dripping with the rain which came out of nowhere on to a sunny beach?' Olive offers.

Rose does not but remembers listening with him to Nina Simone sing 'Summertime' on the radio and the time and effort it took him to help her plant her rosebushes.

Olive recalls their shared delight in the crashing sound of the waves. Then she says, 'I remember the time he cut the toe out of his sock so he could place an injured bird inside it and have its head poke out the through the hole.'

'Frank is gone,' she says, 'his coat is hanging up in my house.'

'Not for me,' says Rose. 'I wonder if life would have been different, though, had he lived– but thinking about this can be so exhausting.'

They have all the time in the world, and they chat across the space Frank once filled and because they don't want to forget him, they sit in the market till they are the only remaining stallholders.

Rose stands up. She doesn't believe what she sees. There is an angel hanging from a rooftop with its wings outspread.

'An angel,' she says.

'I don't see it,' answers Olive.

Rose closes her eyes. 'Is it Edith?' she asks, 'I miss her.'

Pamela walks past them wearing a cloche hat. She has a library to run. She stares as if she hasn't seen them, before waving her handbag and calling out, 'sorry' and 'isn't it a misty day!' when neither Rose nor Olive can see anything misty about the day or a reason why she should be sorry.

'Is Alfred Gorkin with her?' Rose asks.

'He's gone too,' says Olive, 'What happened, by the way?'

'I don't know,' replies Rose, 'I often wonder if he was real.'

'Did you never find out?' asks Olive.

The last shoppers approach to buy jam or roses and Rose thanks them. She and Olive go on to talk about the people in the town: the new librarian, Pamela, who has pulled her cloche hat over her eyes, the minister, who spares no-one his musings on life's meaning and the lady who lives in the yellow house next door to Rose's in a constant state of readiness for war. Mostly, though, they talk about the man who mystified them the most – they talk about Frank and the kind things he did for them.

'I don't miss him' says Rose, 'because his story never leaves me. I have pretended all these years that heis still here – still talking to me - and even if I assembled only a handful of facts about him while he was alive, he is present in everything I do.'

When evening falls over this peculiar town, there is once again little more to hear than distant sea noise and soon there will be little to see because the light weakens and grows thin and pale. Rose holds out her hands as if to grasp the last of the light before it disappears. She faces Olive across a long moment and the unsaid slips into their hearts.

You can quieten words, but not the unsaid, thinks Rose.

'I love you Olive because you are so strange,' she says, feeling something from a part of her life she thought she had long left behind. 'You are my rainbow to keep.'

'What's wrong? Something is wrong,' asks Olive, thinking about the rainbows she keeps in her head.

But it is nothing – just things hovering around Rose's memory like the taste of cake, the salt smell of a room with sea-green curtains, the perfume of roses, the clacking of pebbles pushed by tides, the thumping of a lathe – sights and sounds which are impossible to hold on to.

Does our uncertainty about Frank mean we have become people who can't hold on to anything – ourselves included? Rose thinks.

'Nothing is wrong,' she replies, 'I just miss Frank.'

It's not possible to say everything – if only she had the time. Anyway, where to start and where to stop?

Her throat feels dry and broken and she rises to leave. Here I go again, she thinks, always on the point of leaving, always planning my departure, always in a hurry to get to where I am not.

'We should be heading off now,' she says, 'you never know with roses – new blooms can spring to life while our backs are turned. We can't stay here, anyway.'

'Why not?' asks Olive but she takes her mother's hand, 'here comes the night.'

'The sky is a kind of green,' says Rose.

They walk towards the dying light and Olive holds Rose to stop her falling.

'Thank you,' says Rose who would rather say this than 'goodbye'.

'Thank you,' says Olive who hugs and kisses her mother – something she has not done since Frank died. After this day, Rose will settle in her memory as a curved lady sitting in a market stall wearing a yellow coat and wellington boots and she will know what she has always known – that of all the people who failed her, Rose is one who never would.

'I can't do without your strangeness. I might come and live with you in the house near the rocks,' says Rose, 'but not today,' and off they go to live their lives.

When Rose puts her key in her lock the thought strikes – although it's quickly extinguished, that she wouldn't mind living out her days with Olive. She doesn't expect to have a good time ever again, but she has come to see that not every problem needs to be solved.

You never learn everything about the people you love, anyway. I am safest in my house with my roses and olive tree and hope Olive feels the same way about her home, she thinks.

When Olive returns to her wooden house, she finds that the whole and the broken have revisited. One of her windows has been pushed ajar and the glass smashed, leaving long shards all over the place which crunch beneath her boots.

Her first thought – how foolish she feels –is that it is Eric who has returned and crashed into her home. But there in front of her, and stiff as pokers, are a tawny owl with knowing eyes and matted feathers and its dead partner lying at its feet on her floor made from trees in which they might have slept a few summers before.

Were they confused by the reflections in the glass? she wonders.

'Are you angels?' she asks because the live owl has knowing eyes and because her head is full of angels. 'What can you see about the world that I am missing?'

Might the owl understand things about me I don't? she asks herself.

She thinks she sees the owl wink. She thinks she hears it reply 'life is about not knowing, making the best of things. Some stories are without end.'

But it is just an owl.

She opens her broken window as wide as it can go and throws the dead bird out on to the rocks. She thinks she sees its stricken partner blink back a reprimand before it circles her room and soars out across a full moon to the other side of the bay hoping, perhaps, to surprise another woman through another window.

Then Olive turns her back on the sky because Rose says it is bad luck to stand at a window and look at a full moon. She lies down on her sofa with her arms folded across her chest and waits for the night to do its work.

When Rose hears about the owls, she says 'they are a sign' then starts laughing and can't stop because she doesn't know of what.

And this might be where it's best to leave Rose and Olive because people are people and when you intrude on them too much – even with affection – something almost always gets broken.

In the future, Alfred Gorkin will dream about scenes from his past on the night before he returns to his sister and the country of his birth. He will understand, at last, that he always wanted nothing more or less than to go home and he will tell his sister, 'exile is not for everyone.' She will reply, 'someone had to stay behind to greet you when you returned, and that someone is me.'

Eric won't stop drifting and Pamela will marry the minister who, by then, will no longer be a minister.

Rose's roses will continue to bloom, and Rose will continue to believe in angels until the time when a nightjar flies down and says in Frank's voice, 'it is time to carry you away.'

She will then float into the mystery she has always inhabited – the mystery of Frank.

Olive will have to leave the wooden house near the rocks when the sea pours over everything, dissolving boundaries and turning her part of the town into another friend she has loved and lost. She will move back to the house of her birth and Rose's birth and will stand in wellington boots planting marrows between roses with her strong, beautiful daughter growing inside her because things keep on moving on.